THE ACT(

DECEIT

CW00340995

NELL GREY

Freshwater Bay Series Book 2

COPYRIGHT

The Actor's Deceit
Freshwater Bay, Book 2

Nell Grey

Copyright © 2019 by Nell Grey

Table of Contents

ABOUT NELL

Nell Grey is a full-time writer of romance. She lives in Wales with her husband and two children. When she's not busy writing, she loves to travel and lived in New Zealand for a few years before returning to the UK. A successful career in the corporate world, plus time running restaurants, and teaching in schools, colleges and prisons all make for a rich gumbo of life experiences that help inspire Nell's work. When not writing, she enjoys hiking in the Welsh countryside and hanging out with friends, laughing and sharing stories together. And yes, there's usually wine involved.

FOLLOW NELL GREY

Follow Nell Grey's Facebook page and never miss a story.
https://www.instagram.com/nellgreybooks/
https://twitter.com/NellGrey1
You can email Nell at nellgreybooks@gmail.com

OTHER BOOKS IN THE FRESHWATER BAY SERIES

Book 1 - The *Strictly* Business Proposal- Beth and Gareth
Book 3 - Their Just Deserts - Alys and Owen
Book 4 - The Rural Escape - Jo and Madog

ABOUT THE BOOK

The Freshwater Bay Series continues in Book Two:

The Actor's Deceit - Ariana and Rhys

When washed-up Hollywood actor Rhys Morgan chooses life over death, he realises that he can only fight the demons that are destroying him by returning home to Freshwater Bay, on the remote West Wales coast.

Poor life choices and a failing acting career have left Rhys in crisis, considering what he wants out of life and who he wants to share it with. In his attempt to escape the truth, he's woven himself a tangled web, telling too many lies to too many people, including his one true love. Will he win back the woman who he's wronged the most?

When struggling jewellery designer Ariana Jones realises that her ex, Rhys *The Rat* Morgan, is back home, her world is blown apart. As they spend more time together will she be able to resist his charms? And how will she tell him that she loves another man?

CHAPTER ONE

It was now or never.

He stood shivering, a hundred and fifty feet over the earth below. The four a.m. Sunday morning air was chilled and the Colorado Street Bridge eerily peaceful. Still buzzing from the large line of coke he'd snorted as a final salutation, it hadn't been easy getting over the anti-jump barriers, and he needed the same resolve now to finish this. It was all over and it needed to end now... Now... NOW.

Or never? For Christ's Sake, what was he waiting for?

No matter how he tried, however hard he fixed his resolve to *just fucking do it*, his treacherous fingers still flatly refused to prise their vice-like grip from the railings. They anchored him to the bridge, traitorously ignoring what his head was screaming for them to do, to *please, please* let go and let him fly and be free. Free from this Hell hole, forever.

Finally, after what seemed like an age, his frozen fingers won the fight and his feet rose up too in mutiny, edging their way gingerly back along the ledge and over the chain-linked barriers, back to his abandoned station wagon.

Slamming his defeated head hard against the car window, he groaned in desperation. *Why* hadn't he done it? Had he *ever* actually intended to? He knew the cops would doubt it if they came and booked him now. Loser, he thought. *Fucking amateur*. He'd not even written a note. It'd be just another drink-drive to them.

He sat in the driver's seat and took a swig from the half bottle of Jack in the glove box. Leaning onto the steering wheel, he slumped, his face in his arms, sobbing uncontrollably; broken and alone in a city that would never be his home.

Luc: You there?
Bianca: Luc? You okay?
Luc: I tried to kill myself last night
Bianca: SHIT!!!
Luc: Spent an hour on the side of the Colorado Bridge too chicken shit to jump
Bianca: Oh Luc, baby. Talk to me about it

Luc: Nothing to say. It's all pointless. I tried to end it and I couldn't even manage to do that right
Bianca: I'm so glad. Fuck, Luc! Please tell me you'll never do that again. Can we talk? Facetime? Let me come out to you
Luc: You know the rules
Bianca: How can I help you if I can't see you?
*Luc: You **can** help me*
Bianca: How?
Luc: Tell me why I need to live
Bianca: For me. Live for me
Luc: Why?
Bianca: 'Cos I'm your best friend and I love you. That's why
Luc: I need help to get clean. Then I'll come to you
Bianca: You can do this, Luc
Luc: Maybe?
Bianca: Do it for me. Check into the treatment centre I sent you. Please
...
Bianca: Luc. You still there?
Luc: Yes. I'm hurting like Hell. But still here. I'm going offline now... To call them
Bianca: I'll be waiting for you

Rhys Morgan, cocaine addict, alcoholic, womaniser, deceiver, bit-part actor and recently failed bridge jumper, finally took a leap, this time of faith, and checked himself into a residential treatment centre. And if this didn't work, he told his rebellious fingers sternly as they pressed the door intercom, next time when he stood on that bridge, they *would not* win.

Ariana wiped the tears rolling down her face as she stared at the screen, pushing her unruly hair back as it stuck onto her wet cheek. Why couldn't you talk to me first, she asked the screen, despairing with him and herself. Luc was in so much pain and she was utterly unable to help him. It was all she could do to contain the anger, fear and tears welling up inside her. *Dammit.* He'd got her crying again, she grumbled, as she grabbed a tissue and snapped the laptop shut. And she was so *not* the crying type. In fact, she hadn't cried since she was a teenager. Since Rhys.

7

Ariana had met Luc online. He had a Celtic art website and had started buying pieces from her Freshwater Bay gallery located in a little village on the rugged, wild West Wales coast. She'd been pretty cagey with him at first as she was still raw from being cheated in one of her first deals. It had almost put her out of business, and more than just hurting the bottom line, it had damn near *killed* her pride and self-confidence. The dealer vanished. The Police told her that there was nothing to be done, she should have got him to pay first. She'd been a fool.

So when Luc came along online, she'd insisted strictly on money before shipment. And he'd proved a great contact, restoring *most* of her faith in humanity. He bought mainly small pieces that were easy to post out, particularly Ariana's own range of Celtic jewellery which she designed and made, and were now proving a big hit Stateside.

It began as business, but they had become online pals and started chatting more regularly. She'd used her middle name Bianca for her username and his was Luc, short for Lucentio. She'd guessed he was of Italian descent, like her, or Mexican maybe? Truthfully, she had no idea. She'd never seen or talked face to face to the guy. They'd only type chatted. He'd insisted on it. At first, she'd taken it as a professional decision, but weirdly it became part of their connection. To keep it to just words. Kind of mysterious. It kept her guessing about who he really was.

They'd been talking for well over a year now. He told her he was twenty-eight, same as her, living in Los Angeles. Like so many other wannabes, he'd gone there to break into acting but mainly worked in a bar and did his web business now. Working multiple jobs to earn a crust, like her. And he had proved to be really good at web design and driving up her sales. They both made money from it and she made regular shipments two or three times a week, servicing an American market hungry for Celtic connections.

Once they began chatting more regularly, she could see that he was lonely. His big break into acting had never happened and the Hollywood dream was pretty much a nightmare. She was no expert, but he sounded depressed, and they talked, particularly when he was feeling low. She couldn't just abandon him, especially after he told her about his problems.

Luc had the link to a clinic Ariana had sent him details about. She'd been in touch with them, they knew about him, all he had to do, they said, was to make contact. She hoped with all her heart that he now had.

It was only type chat, but Luc felt as real as anyone she talked with in Freshwater Bay. When he was on form, he was viciously funny. He had an artistic temperament and she loved the way he saw the world.

She'd asked him once,

Bianca: *Tell me about Los Angeles*

He typed back,

Luc: *It's hot and smoggy. Strung-out people and places tied together by traffic-snarled freeways*

Bianca: *What's it like to live there?*

Luc: *It's humanity in a bowl, I guess. You've got your Malibu and Mulholland Drive billionaires living up the road from the Crips and the Bloods. It's a great place if you've got the greenbacks, a hard place if you haven't. It's a magnet for all that's best and all that's worst, with nothing in between*

Bianca: *Tell me about something beautiful there. Here, in Freshwater Bay, we have the sunsets. I sit on a driftwood log on the beach by my house and watch the sun slipping down the sky and melting into the sea.*

He messaged her the next day.

Luc: *You got me thinking. I've never seen the sunrise here. After finishing up work last night, I drove out and hiked up to a place called The Wisdom Tree to catch the dawn. The sun came up like a fireball, so fierce, the whole city turned first pink then a blood orange. It was beautiful, Bianca, the colours here are so vivid, I wish I could take you there someday. Thank you for asking. I'd never have known.*

It sounded magical. Ariana longed to have been there with him.

The fact that she didn't have a clue what Luc looked like worried Rhian, Ariana's best friend. Rhian had known Ariana forever, and when Ariana first told her about Luc, she put her head in her hands and despaired. Typical Ariana, she had such a kind heart, but she was a total sucker for a sob-story.

"I'm not being funny, yeah, but you like this Luc *precisely because* he's halfway across the world," Rhian told her honestly.

"You don't even know what he looks like, Ariana. He could be anybody. A psycho or a serial rapist."

9

"Or... he could look like Ryan Reynolds or Matt Damon," Ariana chirped in.

"Or a Hell's Angel biker with a Mohican and tear tattoos under his eyes for every victim he's killed," Rhian laughed.

"Or super sexy like Bradley Cooper?"

"Or super-*sized* and living in his bed."

"*Enough, alright!* He's my soulmate," Ariana pleaded.

"*Puh-lease!*" Rhian told her straight. "Listen, *space cadet,* stop orbiting Planet Fantasy and get back to Earth. Drop him, and fast. Will's back training with the rugby team again. We could go to the game on Saturday, have a couple of drinks with the boys after. And seeing as you've still got your cute little ass, *unlike me* who is now waddling like a duck, you will have no problem at all in finding yourself a beefy hottie to hook up with."

It was easy for her, thought Ariana miserably. Rhian and Will had been together, rock-solid, since school, now with baby number three on the way. When you get to the ripe old age of twenty-eight, she mused, all the good ones were snapped up and all she seemed to be left with these days were the desperados. The recently divorced and randy as Hell, or the players who had no intention of a lasting relationship. Why was it all so complicated? No, as much as she loved Rhian and Will, she'd rather not spend Saturday night with drunken rugby playing brutes slobbering into her ear and trying to grope her at the bar.

Most of those boys, anyway, had been at high school with her and had teased and made fun of her, until she was seventeen when all of a sudden they began asking her out. And she'd picked Rhys *the Rat* Morgan, the best-looking boy in the school, not because of that, but because he'd held her hand when she was scared in a boat on a school Art trip.

Her judgement had been dodgy back then. She hoped that it wasn't now with Luc. But... *really!* Her heart and head screamed at her, Luc had *so many* issues. *And* he was five thousand miles away, *and then* she didn't know if she'd be physically attracted to him. *Plus,* last night there was the *tiny* issue that he'd tried to fling himself off a *frickin'* bridge. And if that all wasn't enough, he'd now gone and disappeared offline. Yeah, maybe her judgement *was* out, *just a tad.*

Ariana shook herself and got changed into her restaurant uniform. She had the front of house to run tonight. Beth Morgan, Ariana's friend, owned La Galloise, a French restaurant that sat on the cliff above Freshwater Bay, and which, under Beth, was gaining a reputation as the best place to eat in the area.

Beth, who was heavily pregnant, was meant to be taking it easy. But *her* idea of slowing down was to do twelve-hour rather than fifteen-hour shifts. Gareth, her husband, kept telling her to not be such a control freak and to trust Paul, her very capable deputy. Beth had done well to build a strong team around her at the restaurant in the eighteen months they had been open. Like everything in Freshwater Bay, it had a hectic summer tourist season, and a much quieter winter when the place rattled from the battering wind and rainstorms rolling in straight off the Irish Sea.

Pulling herself together, Ariana fixed her makeup in her bedroom mirror. She carefully applied her lipstick and brushed her hair back into a ponytail. That would have to do, she thought as she looked at her reflection. The last thing Beth needed was Ariana depressed and puffy eyed over some suicidal Yank she'd never even met.

But try as she may, Ariana couldn't shake him out of her head and Luc was still on her mind as she was getting ready to leave the cottage to go to work. She checked her watch. She could still make the post if she hurried.

Rushing back upstairs she opened her dressing table drawer. In there, was a velvet pouch with a pair of rings she'd made recently when she was thinking about Luc. She held and studied them in her palm. She'd deliberately fashioned the most powerful Celtic symbols she could for these rings. The heart and hands of friendship, faith and loyalty from the Claddagh design wrapped into the eternal love of the Welsh Celtic knot in the band. She knew what she had to do. Luc *so* needed this ring now.

Dear Luc,

Stay Strong.

Love Bianca x

She wrote the quick note and placed the larger ring back into the velvet pouch and into a padded envelope for posting. On the front, she copied down the treatment centre address from her phone. For the attention of Luc's Celtic Art Company. She hoped he'd get it. And that he *had* checked in. It was a long shot, but she was an optimist.

She put the other ring on her finger. She'd wear hers. Who knows, it might keep them connected, she hoped. She grabbed the parcel and jogged along the cliff-top path to Freshwater Bay, praying that Tommy

11

Shop, the owner of the village's only general store and post office hadn't decided to close early again.

CHAPTER TWO

"Hi. I'm Rhys. Where do I start? Coke addict, alcoholic, general fuck up. It's my seventh day sober. And it's still a bitch."

"Hey, Rhys."

The group slouching around him in the padded chair circle mumbled their greetings. The group leader called the meeting to a start and Rhys slid down further into his seat too, trying to keep under her radar. He was in no hurry to share.

Most of his time so far at rehab had been spent going through interminable questionnaires, undertaking medical tests, attending therapy sessions and watching hours of television in his room. Being tortured by daytime TV seemed to be part of his cold turkey regime. He sweated and clucked through the dramas and soaps, his depression deepening when he recognised some of the parts that *he'd* auditioned for. Surely, he was a better actor than those goons?

And he had no phone at the clinic. They'd taken all his tech off him so he couldn't make contact with the outside world. *Man*, he would kill for a line of snow right now.

"Rhys, wanna tell the group how this started for you?"

The group therapy leader was eyeballing him intently.

Rhys looked around hoping she was going to let him off the hook, but she bore down on him like a Bruce Lee Ninja. She must have known he'd tuned out when the tight faced woman across from him had started yacking on about her opioid addiction, how it started with a Fentanyl patch for her bad back and then… yadi-yadi-ya… he'd drifted.

Busted. Now he was back in the room and the scary group leader with the dyed orange hair was poised and ready to pounce, to slit him open with her stare and get him to spill his guts out to the group. Surely, an actor of his calibre could muster an appropriate performance of snivelling, wailing and regret, he pondered? He could and should make up something appropriately tragic. A real tearjerker. Because who *really* would care about *his* story? But instead, he chose to squirm and stare down at the floor in silence, with everyone still looking at him. Waiting.

"Rhys?"

"*Uhhh*... how it started?" he cleared his throat as he spoke.

What was he going to say? How *had* it started? Smoking weed in the boathouse, his dad's old shed, tucked out of sight, down by the rocks at the back of Freshwater Bay. Then moving on to doing lines of coke at the weekend with his mates in the Lobster Pot Inn toilets.

It started by getting high. Coke gave him confidence and energy beyond anything he'd known before. A line of white and the world was at his feet. *God*, he'd loved it *so much* back then. He did more and more, *and then some*. In London at Drama School. Here, when he first came to Los Angeles five years before.

As his habit increased, the insomnia started; then came the anxiety, the insecurities and a terrifying first panic attack in a Target store. He'd started to hit the drink more too in L.A. He needed that to bring him back down. The drink made all the time he spent alone more bearable.

"*Ah man…* It started way back. At home and then Drama School. Dabbling. Partying. That kinda thing."

He deflected the question, still not making eye contact, praying that they would take that for an answer and leave him alone.

Where had it started? Ariana's revenge.

He'd started hanging out with some choice guys in school and Ariana had bitched about it, telling him how bored she was sitting with them in the boathouse watching them pass bongs around all night, getting high.

They'd been going out for a few weeks when he took her to the Prom. He could still picture her now in that scarlet dress and her hair, like silky chocolate, pinned up with curls tumbling down. It still left him breathless to think of her, and how he was such a dumbass, ditching her as soon as he got there. He stood at the bar all night drinking with the boys or doing lines in the bogs, while she danced with her friend, Rhian.

Fuelled by the coke, he bet his mates big bucks he could get Ariana on video *doing it* with him. Up to now, she'd been a total cock tease and it was high time she finally put out for him, he'd decided.

He wandered over to her; she was sitting at a table near the dancefloor with her friends.

He whispered in her ear, "Ari, let's split. I've got a surprise for you. But you've got to come with me."

Her eyes lit up and he got her to the bar area before she started asking questions.

"No *way* am I doing that!"

At first, she flatly refused to go with him to the room upstairs that he'd booked.

"Ah come on, Ari, sweetie," he charmed her, "I want you so badly. It will be so good. Trust me, honey."

"But Rhys, how could you do this without even asking me?"

She started getting pissy with him, but he kissed her hard on the mouth, taking her breath away and making her hot in ways he knew he could, doing everything in his powers to coax her into the elevator and then up to the room. And by her actions, once he'd lured her into the lift, she was no angel either. He could tell she was up for it too.

"Sorry I... I just need a minute," Ariana said, rushing into the bathroom and locking the door firmly behind her. Her nerves had begun to get the better of her as soon as she was in the room and had seen the bed.

Rhys, taking his chance, quickly lined up his camera on the side-table and set it to record. Then he waited for Ariana, sitting on the Victorian iron frame bed of that God-awful chintzy room that had cost him a small fortune. Bored, he stretched out, batting the stacked pointless cushions onto the floor. He was convinced he'd blown it. She was so quiet in there. He'd have to pay out serious cash to the boys if he didn't get this video.

"Ari? Come out of the bathroom, babe, and *talk* to me. I'm *lonely*," he coaxed.

A few moments later she emerged, stripped down to her strapless bra and panties. He stared at her speechless. He'd been laid a good few times already, but he was dazzled by the sight of her long body and her smooth, olive skin. She was perfection. It didn't take much persuading, Ariana soon had *him* stripped too. He was naked on the bed, and by the look of him, she could tell that he was *more* than ready for her.

"Ari, what you doing?" he asked her.

The red light on his camera she'd noticed when she walked out of the bathroom had shocked her. She'd been working herself up to gain the courage to do this. Rhys was meant to be her first, but now she could see that all the time he'd been planning to *secretly video her*.

The rat!

Her only way out of unwittingly becoming the co-star in Rhys' homemade porn movie, she realised in that moment, was to dig deep and to channel her own Oscar-winning performance.

She whispered into his ear, teasing him, "Rhys, I've been dreaming about this. I've been fantasising that when we do it, I get to be in control. Tie you up. Make you my slave."

His high-octane coke-fuelled body was so fired up for *that*.

"Oh God, baby, okay, whatever you want. *Yeah*."

She picked up his necktie and went to retrieve the sash belt of her dress. Then straddling on top of him, she fastened him securely to the bed's iron headrails. She moved off him again and reached over to his trousers, strewn below him on the bed.

"Ari, good thinking. I've a rubber in my wallet. You'll need to put it on me, baby."

Instead of the wallet though, she fished out a small plastic bag of white powder from his back pocket and dropped it on his stomach.

"*Ahh*. I saved some for us," he said hopefully, though he knew Ariana never did drugs.

She'd suspected what he'd been up to all evening, and now here was the evidence.

"Yeah, right."

Her tone was flat, and she was now focussed directly on the camera on top of the side-table, pointing at the bed.

Rhys saw her staring at it.

"*Shit!* Ariana! I can explain."

She looked at him hatefully as she reached for her clutch bag, took out her mobile phone and snapped him, helpless, tied to the bed, buck naked and erect for all the world to laugh at, with a bag of blow on his belly.

Ariana listened to him from the bathroom as she got dressed. He was snivelling and banging against the bed, trying to free himself. Throwing him a cold, disparaging glare as she came back into the bedroom, she casually ignored his pitiful pleas to untie him.

"We are *so* over," she sneered at him as she left, slamming the bedroom door shut behind her.

That night, late, she shared the picture online with all her school friends whilst Rhys was still tied to the bed, shouting for help, unaware that he'd been publicly shamed. Housekeeping unfastened him next morning.

With all his school pals resharing it and generally ripping the shit out of him about the picture, he stayed well clear of Freshwater Bay and spent the summer before drama school, when he wasn't filming, hanging out in Holyguard with the guys, stoned out of his skull most of the time.

"So how did the dabbling get out of control, Rhys?" the Ninja group leader drilled into him.

Rhys looked around the circle of his group, sulkily making full eye contact with them for the first time. He really wasn't in the mood for this.

"I guess you mix drugs and drink up with a whole heap of insecurities and this is what you get."

Rhys gestured at himself pompously, "A Class A fuck up."

"Bullshit!"

An aggressive voice in the group called him out. They weren't being brushed off with that crock of shit. This guy wasn't selling that to them. He had deep issues and he needed to get over himself.

"Why you hate yourself so much, dude?"

A hollow-eyed, young emo with rings on his lip and eyebrow was staring at him from the circle at two o'clock.

"Yeah, man. Everything starts somewhere. Where was it with you?"

Were they trying to help him? What did they know?

Rhys stared around the circle at the faces all looking his way. This was starting to get uncomfortable. He felt angry. They were pushing him. Was he *really* going to go there?

"Okay. You got me."

He treated them to one of his winning smiles. The kind he'd used all his life when he wanted something.

Deadpan faces. It was like he'd suddenly lost his superpowers. He ran his hand through his hair.

"I guess everything is about me screwing up big time. That's where it started."

He took a deep breath, some of them seemed a little kinder but this was definitely the toughest gig he'd ever played.

"My career's a total failure but I've told everyone, my family, my friends, that I've made it big."

The group leader nodded at him to keep going.

"My mother thinks I'm rubbing shoulders with the stars, right? Taking lead parts. Her wonderful son is a hotshot Hollywood A-lister, not some two-bit extra who's only played a Soviet guard and third customer in a coffee shop in the last six months. I work in a downtown bar while she's revving herself up for her invite to the *frickin'* Oscars."

17

He stared down at his trainers, mumbling, "And I don't know how to stop the lies."

The tears were threatening to come. His eyes burned. *Shit!* He was determined that he was *not* going to blub. He fought it back. Not here. Not in front of strangers.

"*So?* Put it right, dude. Tell 'em the truth."

The young emo seemed dismissive of his predicament.

Rhys knew it sounded so silly when he said it like that. Like it was something that could just be forgiven and fixed. Patched up. They didn't get how many years were invested in this dream, not least by his mother, and how hurt his family would be if they saw what he really was. A total fraud. A pitiful loser. An addict. How could they forgive all those lies? How could *he* ever look them straight in the eye? How would they ever believe a word he said again?

"Yeah right."

Rhys slumped back angrily. He sniffed and swallowed down a hard lump of emotion. He'd shared enough. And a fat lot of good it had done him. They didn't understand. He squeaked his chair loudly, pushing it back as he rushed out of the room as soon as the meeting ended. How many more days of this *crap* would he have to put up with?

He checked in at the front office. He wasn't sure why. No one knew he was in rehab, but he still had a need to connect with the outside world. He resolved to ask for his phone back, make an excuse that he needed it to call his mother in Wales. Looking at the workbench, it seemed to be a dumping ground for letters and files, maybe phones too?

He scanned the desk; over to the side to him was a small parcel, a padded envelope. It was addressed to *his* company. Strange. Only Ariana knew he was here. It was lying on the desk, presumably about to be returned to sender.

"*Hey*. That's *my* company. Celtic Art."

He picked up the parcel and opened it.

"Sorry. Gotta check it first, Rhys."

The support worker in the office moved from a computer station and examined the envelope for contraband. It contained only a velvet pouch. Ariana had sent him a ring. And inside, there was a small card attached.

Dear Luc,
Stay Strong.

Love Bianca x

The ring was beautiful, he thought as he held it up and examined it closely. It was silver with an intricate Celtic knot design worked all around the band. At the front was a gold heart with silver hands around it. He recognised it immediately as a Claddagh ring. Ariana had sold a few of these before, but she'd never made the heart with gold, or with this intricate Celtic love-knot banding. It was exquisite. He slipped it onto his right ring finger. It fitted exactly with the heart pointing at his.

The support worker studied the ring too.

"That's *cute*."

"Yeah, my friend makes them. She's real talented," Rhys said proudly, "Can I get my phone back, I need to call my mom in Wales?"

It wasn't true but it was worth a shot to try and arrange a drop-off. A little line, that's all he needed. Just one sniff to help him deal with this poxy place.

"You have a family emergency?"

"*Uh*... not that I know of."

"Not a chance then, sorry."

And that was that.

Walking slowly back to his room, even though he tried his best to distract himself, he couldn't stop thinking about Ariana. Thinking about Ariana got him through the day, he realised. And now she'd sent him the ring. He kept playing with it, moving it on his finger. She'd made this for him. It was so beautiful. Just like her.

She was always so talented in the Art class they shared. He remembered their field trip out across Freshwater Bay to one of the islands to sketch the seabirds. They hit some big waves on the way back and he'd held Ariana's hand tightly as they bumped through them. It was her first time in a fishing boat, and she was scared. He'd asked her out when they got to the shore and he remembered how his heart thumped when she said yes.

"So, let's get back to this anger you say you feel inside you, Rhys."

The one to one counselling was helping, but with twenty days sober, Rhys was exhausted. He was feeling more clear-headed, but the demons were still weighing heavy. Every day he seemed to have more headspace to reflect. The therapy and counselling helped raise things that were buried but needed to be dealt with, and he spent most of his time between sessions processing and reflecting.

He began to walk in the gardens and get out of his room more often. It was helping him to think, to consider what was important to him, what he wanted to do with his life. He was at a crossroads. But this was no fork in the road; it felt like he'd been thrown out of a plane. He was in free fall, hurtling towards the earth. But now at least, he rationalised, he had a clear view of the ground he was going to hit. He just hoped he'd find the parachute cord soon.

By now, he could get through the day without thinking too much about coke. The booze was more of a challenge. He still thought about that constantly. The denial made the craving worse. *Boy,* what he would do for a slam or two of tequila to take the edge off how he was feeling.

"Tell me about the photo you mentioned. The one that you're embarrassed about. That you identified as a trigger."

His counsellor, Greg, sat opposite him as Rhys leaned back in the armchair. A box of tissues sat on the table between them, a nonverbal signal to let it all out. No way was he going to be needing those.

"*Uhh...* Rhys? The photo?"

He nodded for him to start talking about it.

"Yeah, the photo. What's to say about that? My stupid past. No one *says* anything. But I know the photo's still out there. If you search hard enough, you can see *all* of me *and my drugs* in glorious technicolour, you know what I'm saying? The casting agents know about it too, I think. So it screws my chances before I even audition."

"*Really?* How do you feel about it?"

Rhys looked away. How *did* he feel?

"I feel pissed!"

That wasn't quite right. What he felt had been a chromatic scale, a glissando of emotions. Hate and anger sliding into guilt and shame, and by now it had become something else.

But he'd started out *real* angry. He'd wanted to crush Ariana and destroy any success she might enjoy too. Make her feel the pain that he'd felt.

"I wanted to make her pay. Big time. It didn't work though... Just made me feel worse."

"What did you do, Rhys?" the counsellor probed, worried in case he'd harmed this girl.

"I heard she'd started a new art gallery, so I tried to ruin her," Rhys explained quietly, rubbing his face.

He had set up a fake business name, social media profile and new email address and posed as a London art dealer.

"It was the easiest thing. She was so gullible; I took five thousand pounds worth of art off her upfront in her first big deal."

She agreed for him to pay within fourteen days of delivery, but she never got a penny. A drama school friend had picked it up from a London collection point and shipped it on for him to a parcel locker in San Francisco. He flew out there on a sightseeing trip and picked it up. Home and dry. He then quickly deleted all traces of the fake business.

"I crippled her cash flow in one fell swoop, then sold the lot."

He looked up at Greg.

"It's all there, sitting in an account. 'Cos I felt so bad after, I invested it and tripled her money. I could give it to her now, but things have gone too far between us."

He wasn't proud of what he'd done. Besides it was a criminal act, she could call the police, convict him. What had possessed him to do it? Was it another symptom of his cocaine-fogged mind? He was working on not blaming the blow for his actions. But truthfully, it hadn't helped.

"It's done and I can't undo it. I just wish I could go back to before the lies."

He looked at the clock. *Dammit,* he still had half the session to go. *Bollocks to it.* He decided to get it all off his chest.

"And if that wasn't bad enough, after that, I cheated her again. I created another character. This time, I became Luc, the screwed up American art dealer. I was trying to get her attention and get her to start talking to me again."

"Did it work?"

"Yeah, you could say that. She's totally in love with him and I feel a total asshole about it every time we talk."

Greg put his pen down and stared intently at Rhys, trying to get his around what he'd just said.

"Why Luc?" he asked finally.

"Cos I'm a pretentious actor prick, *that's why.*"

Gus raised an eyebrow.

Rhys explained, "She used her middle name, Bianca in her online account, so I gave Bianca her Lucentio."

Gus still looked blankly at Rhys.

"Taming of the Shrew, *man*. You know? *The play!* I was using another guy to get my girl."

He still looked blank. Gus was obviously not a Shakespeare fan.

"Did you steal from her again?"

"No. I sold her stuff honestly from then on, and she insisted on money upfront."

He smirked at Gus, "I make more on the web sales now than on acting jobs. Did a college course in web design and sales and everything. Turns out, I'm a regular *frickin'* entrepreneur."

"So, how are things with her now?" Greg pushed.

"Honestly? It's killing me," Rhys finally admitted. "We talk online a lot. I get so lonely. Especially at night, after work. She's so sweet. She really cares so much for me, it hurts. I beat myself up so bad after that I just wanna get wasted. *Shit*!"

Rhys bent forward, head in his hands, "I'm twenty-eight years old. I should be raising Hell, not sitting home boozing until dawn like some old, fucking lush."

The counsellor looked on impassively.

"But going out, clubbing, hooking up. It bores me, man. Nothing's real, except *her*, and everything I've told *her* is a lie. Including who I am…"

Rhys paused, eyeballing the counsellor bitterly.

So how are things now, Greg? I'd say that things *now* are *pretty fucked up*, wouldn't you?"

An uncomfortable silence descended. It was too much and at last Rhys cracked. His anger ebbing away, his defences drowned, he burst open, breaking down and weeping hard, his hand covering his eyes.

"Let it out, Rhys. It's okay."

"It's not okay," he answered despairingly. "I love her and she's pretty much the only girl I've ever wanted. And the *fucking* irony of it is, she's the one I can *never* have. She's too good for me. Of everyone, I've deceived her the most. *I know her*, and when she finds out, she'll hate me forever."

Rhys laughed resignedly through his tears, "I've gone and written myself the starring role in this tragedy, *right*?"

By his face, he thought, Greg pretty much agreed. The time was up.

"Rhys, we're making progress, but we need to talk about this some more."

CHAPTER THREE

"I *love* that ring."

It was the first thing Beth noticed.

"Thanks. It's a new design I've made," Ariana answered dreamily.

She sat with Ariana in one of the empty navy leather booths of La Galloise restaurant drinking lattes. They'd been meaning to catch up for ages. Ariana was helping her out by working more evening shifts as Beth got closer to the baby's due date. Beth was blooming but she'd be glad when Junior finally made an appearance. The extra weight on her small frame was tiring her out each day. And a commercial kitchen was not designed to deal with heavily pregnant women. It was hot as Hell and a busy, tight squeeze when everyone was working at their stations. Twice this week she'd covered herself in sauce. She wasn't used to being this big. She needed foam bumper bars around her. But it was Ariana she was concerned about now. She'd agreed to help out but she was now upping her shifts even more.

"Are you sure that you're not overdoing it, Ariana? Working here evenings and doing your jewellery all day?"

Ariana didn't tell her that she could really do with the money right now. Luc hadn't sold any of her pieces for a month and her sales had flatlined. She was worried about how long she could last and prayed things would pick up once the tourist season started. There was no way she was telling Beth that. She knew she'd help her out if she needed it, but her pride would never let her ask. Things would work out, she told herself. They always did.

Ariana reassured her, "No, 'course not, it's what I've always done, worked in the evening. It gets me out. Otherwise, I'd be stuck at home watching the soaps with Gwen,"

She'd been working evenings in the Lobster Pot Inn when Beth had first come to Freshwater Bay. At the time, it was the only place in the village to eat and stay. Beth, a talented chef from London, had inherited La Galloise restaurant, at the time standing empty on the cliff tops above, and had fallen in love with architect Gareth Morgan, the eldest son of a well-known local farming family. Together they had transformed the restaurant and built a chalet complex for local housing and tourist rentals. With Beth's talent and acumen, business was booming.

"Tell me more about this ring you've made," Beth asked curiously.

Ariana grinned.

"It's one of my special Celtic ones," she winked at Beth.

Gareth had given Beth one of Ariana's Celtic rings when they'd gotten married.

Ariana had been friends with Gareth for years. She'd known him when she was going out with his brother, Rhys. She knew the whole family. The four boys, his indomitable mother Ellen, and David, his reticent, deep thinking father. It was a small community and Ellen called round to see Gwen, her gran, from time to time. As Ariana told Beth when she met him, she'd lucked out getting Gareth. Rhys was a total jerk, although Ellen *and Gwen* still thought the sun shone out of his posterior. Gwen occasionally told her what he was up to. He'd bought an apartment by the beach and was filming in New York. Very successful, apparently. Ariana had yet to see him in any of the Netflix films she watched.

"So, any men in your life at the moment?" Beth asked her impishly, "I've got a new chef starting soon; he's single."

"No thanks. Chefs are all as mad as snakes," Ariana replied, smashing Beth's matchmaking efforts swiftly away.

Beth feigned mock outrage and then paused.

"Actually, that is true, except for Paul."

Ariana looked nervously at her spoon. She needed some advice and Beth was always so realistic about things, she knew she'd give her some perspective. She plunged in.

"Beth, you know the guy I talked to you about, the one I was chatting online to?"

"The American art dealer, you mean?"

"Yeah. Him. We've been talking a lot over the last few months."

"Yeah, you said."

Beth's face clouded over.

"Isn't he a bit messed up?"

"Mmm, you could say that. He tried to kill himself the other night."

Beth looked at Ariana, concerned. What was she doing getting involved with a nut job like this? He could be anyone, and Ariana was so naive at times. She was an easy mark. Beth was worried.

"He's not asked you for money or anything, has he?"

She'd been reading a news story about women who got conned out of thousands by men who they mistakenly fell in love with online. The men sold them a sob-story about a fake crisis to get them to send cash.

"No. Nothing like that. But he has got some *problems*," she admitted.

"Problems? What kind?"

"He's lonely. It's usually late at night over there when we talk. I think he's depressed."

Ariana screwed up her nose as Beth looked at her steadily.

"Okay, so he's got a bit of a coke habit too and he drinks too much."

Beth looked at her alarmed.

"Ariana!"

Beth put her hand on Ariana's arm.

"Be careful. He sounds like he needs someone who's there with him, not here in Wales."

"I know. He's gone into rehab, I think. I sent him a ring like this one to send him some positive vibes and stuff."

"That's great. But there can't be a future in it, Ariana. You know that, right?"

Ariana did know. In her heart, she'd known all along that no good would come of her online chats with Luc. But he was like *her* addiction. It was a negative relationship. It stopped her from meeting other people. She'd not dated in over a year. He was her obsession. How ridiculous was *that* when she didn't know what he looked like? What if she didn't find him attractive? That terrified her. She was drawn to his wit and sensitivity. She loved his quirky observations about life. He had an artistic soul. He encouraged her to read books she'd never have tried, mainly American authors; Pynchon and Burroughs, Heller and Vonnegut. Ariana didn't understand everything in them but saw similarities to her favourite postmodern art.

Now he'd gone offline, she was definitely in cold turkey. How could she be in love with a man she'd never even seen? It was crazy; but Ariana couldn't help how she felt.

Rhys packed boxes. Shipping home boxes. Thrift shop boxes. He didn't have much in the shipping pile. There was not much he wanted to keep. Some designer clothes, his favourite books and his vinyls, that was about it. The car, the TV, the sofa, the fridge, anything of value was sold. It was so liberating, walking out of here with nothing much, travelling light. Cutting free.

He would be forever grateful to Ariana for giving him the encouragement to check into rehab. He felt like a sea mist was finally lifting from his mind, the sun pouring out of the clouds. For the first time in years, he felt optimistic again *and* healthy. He was over a month clean, he was eating and sleeping properly; he'd even started running again. But now, best of all, he had a plan forming in his brain. Not all the details were there yet. It was more like a direction of travel that he planned to take.

The plan had started forming a week or so ago when his friends in the group meeting had rounded on him squarely. They'd become closer as the days had gone on. They were a bunch of screw-ups, just like him, but a finer bunch he would struggle to find.

They supported him when he finally told them his greatest shame, stealing from Ariana. And they'd kindly, but honestly, shown him up for being the self-absorbed bastard he really was. They called him out on lots of things. Including using the naked photo as an excuse all these years for his crappy career and piss-poor attitude.

No one had ever been this honest with him. He'd walked all over everyone all his life, he now realised to his shame. He'd been Mam's little blue-eyed boy. Thinking back, he'd been a precocious little brat. After winning a drama competition, he was spotted by a television producer and from there he made it big as a teenage actor on a soap. He remembered being mobbed in Cardiff by fans wanting selfies with him. They'd laugh if they saw him now, making Dirty Martinis in an L.A. bar; just another failed actor in a city that spat them out like cherry stones.

But it was his buddy, Marvin, in group therapy, who'd finally got him smelling the coffee. Marvin, a middle-aged meth head with rotten teeth, who'd told even *more* lies than him. He asked him straight up, eyeballing him,

"What is it, man? Cut the bullshit. What do you really want out of your life?"

That'd made him think. He was only twenty-eight for Christ's Sake. He could do *anything* he wanted. He didn't *have* to keep treading water in this Tinseltown swamp.

His answer was simple.

"I wanna do workshops with the kids again."

After Drama School, he did a stint performing Shakespeare around youth venues. They were the *best* times. Sure, they'd lived out of a van and moved from place to place, it was pretty basic, but it was worth it when they did the workshops with kids who were in gangs, who were bullied, who were struggling with relationships.

Marvin clamped a hand on Rhys' shoulder and told him,

"No more regrets. No more lies. Just do it, dude."

To thine own self be true, Rhys thought. Like Hamlet, he was learning *that* lesson the hard way.

The treatment centre had tried to get him a sponsor but Rhys was going home to Wales. He committed to going to AA meetings in his nearest town and to finding a sponsor there. He was heading to Freshwater Bay for now, and then probably to London, or on the road, he had no idea. But he felt liberated by the possibilities.

And who would have thought it? It turned out that the group therapy worked for him too. At first, he'd been a bit actor*ish* and tried to play characters, take a position, put up blocks. But, the guys in rehab had taken no crap from him. They'd seen him coming and soon stripped that away. As his mam used to say, you can't kid a kidder.

"Owen you there?" Rhys typed into his laptop.

He mentally worked out the time difference. He needed a sponsor. He didn't need an ex-dope head; what he needed was someone to listen, to be there for him. No judgements, just a safety net. Only one person fitted that bill. His brother, Owen.

"Alright, Rhys. How's it going?"

"Need your help, Owen. Can we chat?"

They flipped to the video link; the connection was holding.

"I've just got out of rehab, mate. I'm clean now but I'm done with this place. I'm coming home. Can you help me?" Rhys ventured tentatively.

It was his first time being truthful. How would his brother take it? Owen stared at the screen. He was just out of the shower and sitting in a changing room in a towel.

"Rehab?" Owen bristled, rubbing the back of his neck.

"Yeah. What can I say? The coke and booze finally caught up with me. Had a bit of a moment on a bridge a few weeks back."

His shoulders dropped.

Owen could tell his brother was putting on a good act for him but he was pretty broken.

"Rhys. Talk to me, alright? Tell me about it," he said, trying to reach out over the distance between them.

Owen Morgan, international rugby player, when not playing and training was studying sports psychology and in the last throes of his doctoral studies. He wasn't a counsellor, but Rhys knew, if anyone could help him, it would be him. Plus, he wouldn't blab. He'd trust his brother with his life.

"Owen, I've been in a pretty dark place, man. I just couldn't see the point of it anymore. *Fuck!*"

"We're all here for you, Rhys. Come home. We can help you heal."

"I guess," Rhys agreed tentatively.

"I'm trying, Owen. Every day. Trying to keep a routine. It's hard y'know. They say I need a sponsor. To keep me clean when I'm back home. Will you do it?" he winced, hoping he would agree.

Owen looked at him steadily on screen, "Yeah, no worries. *Of course, I will*, you daft sod."

Rhys breathed a jagged sigh of relief.

Owen studied Rhys' face on his phone screen. What was his little brother going through? He looked like he'd lost weight. His blue eyes still had the same mischievous twinkle that drove their Mam mad and the girls crazy, but there were shadows under them now. They looked haunted.

"Want me to come out? I can make a few calls and be there in a couple of days?" Owen offered.

"No. I've booked a ticket. I'm coming home next week. I just need someone I can trust to talk to. You know, if it gets too much. To help me keep sober."

" Of course, Rhys. Anything. Yes."

"Tidy."

Rhys looked intensely at the screen.

"Owen, I've told so many lies, mate. I need to start telling the truth and I don't know where to start."

He paused; relieved, choked with emotion, "But this feels good."

"Start by coming home." Owen's voice caught as he said it.

Rhys nodded. There was no need for words. He knew he was hurting everyone he loved. It was hard and he felt so helpless.

"You're doing the right thing. Call me day or night, you hear? Anything at all. I'm here for you, bro."

Rhys smiled weakly, ended the call and broke down. He'd told his first person and it felt like the floodgates opening, overwhelming him with relief, but also fear.

Owen clicked off the call on his phone, his eyes darting around the changing room. No one had been taking any notice of him. It had been another gruelling, training session in the middle of the International season. Getting selected for next week's match had been all he was thinking about. And then Rhys had called. He wished he could be there now. Nothing else mattered. How long would it take on a plane to get there? He'd gladly give up his place in the team to go and be there for his little brother. But there was no point. He wouldn't make it soon enough and Rhys would be home next week.

Two peas in a pod. Owen had always been closer to his brother Rhys than to his eldest brother, Gareth or his youngest, Madog. And even though they did totally different things, acting and elite sport, Owen the psychologist understood that they were more similar than most people realised. For Rhys, his motivation had been impressing his friends, partying and playing. Getting the best roles, being the star. For Owen it had been being the star on the sports field, getting selected to play for his team and country, being the fittest athlete. Relentless training. Going harder than anyone else. Pushing your body to the limit, time and time again. The same compulsive, addictive behaviour; just different channels. And it had finally caught up with Rhys. He sent up a prayer. *Stay safe, little brother and come home to us soon.*

CHAPTER FOUR

"Lunch'll be ready in five minutes," Ariana called out from the kitchen to Gwen who was outside getting the garden ready for planting. The wind was blowing off the sea and it was still cold and very muddy, but it would soon be time to put the first potatoes in. Ariana was making them both an omelette.

"*Okey dokey.* Be there now in a minute," Gwen called back.

The cottage was a traditional Welsh stone longhouse with gardens front and back, enough space for Gwen to grow fruit, flowers and veggies all summer, for her bees to buzz around, and for her chickens to scratch about in. The cottage was a mile clifftop walk from Freshwater Bay and sat at the side of a hidden cove on the coastal path looking out at the sea. When the sun shone, it was heaven on earth, a slice of golden sand sheltered by the sheer rock faces of the cliffs. But this was Wales, and the calm days were punctuated by the wet ones that battered the cottage and drove staccato drumbeats of rain horizontally onto the windows.

All around the kitchen, littered across the worktops and lining the shelves of the huge antique dresser were bottle upon bottle of glass kilner jars, full of petals and herbs. Basil, rose, lavender, geranium, rosemary, calendula and many more; all labelled and steeped in almond or olive oil.

Arian thought the place looked like a witch's lair or a madwoman's laboratory. Gwen added these oils to the beeswax that she gathered through the summer from her hives, to make the most wonderful face and lip balms which she sold to tourists and for charity fundraisers.

"*Ugh*, I hate this time of the year," Ariana shivered as Gwen came in from outside.

"It looks like it's going to chuck it down again."

"The rain makes you appreciate the sunshine more, cariad," Gwen placated.

Ariana groaned. She'd gladly be less appreciative and have a bit more sun.

"Hope we can get that round of golf in this afternoon," Gwen said, washing her hands and sitting down at the kitchen table.

Ariana raised an eyebrow.

"Golf? Since when did *you* play golf?"

"*Ed* said I should give it a go. He's bringing his Big Bertha with him to see how well I can drive," she said, waiting for Ariana to bite, which she did immediately, much to Gwen's amusement.

"Who's *Ed*?"

Ariana put their omelettes on the table along with a salad she'd made.

"My new boyfriend," Gwen said with a cheeky grin. " He lost his wife last year."

Gwen took her plate and started helping herself to the salad.

"Retired?"

"Kind of. He owns a string of funeral parlours up and down the coast."

Ariana stopped chewing.

"Don't look at me *like that.* Anyway, he's my toyboy. He's only seventy. Plus he's offered me a discount when I pop my clogs."

"Gran! You're seventy-nine.

"Precisely."

Ariana rolled her eyes. There was obviously still plenty of life in the old chook yet.

Gwen, who'd taught in the village school for years, knew just about everyone, so there'd be a fair bit of gossip about Ed once word got out. She was Ariana's grandmother on her father's side. Ariana's mother was Italian Welsh, a second-generation family who made and sold ice cream. Ariana had come along unexpectedly when her parents were just out of their teens. She was a love child; Gwen told her kindly. It had been quite a scandal in the village at the time.

Her parents had both worked then and now on the Irish ferry on two-week rotations, so Ariana spent most of her childhood with Gwen, whose husband died of a heart attack at a young age. By the time Ariana reached high school, she more or less lived there. It made sense with her parents' work patterns, but she always felt like she'd always been an unexpected inconvenience to them. It stung Ariana that Gwen had been more of a mother to her than her real one. When her parents moved to Ireland, she'd chosen to stay. How could she leave Gwen or this view?

"Your dad called again last night. Wanted to know when you're going over to see them," she reminded Ariana.

"I can't Gwen, I'm skint."

She hadn't told her gran how badly her sales had dropped but Gwen seemed to sense that there was a problem.

31

"You still using the studio?" Gwen suggested. "You could try putting it online to make some cash in the summer as a tourist rental?"

"Maybe," Ariana considered. It wasn't a bad idea, although it was in a bit of a state. She didn't like to go in because of the monster spiders in there.

When Ariana came back from her jewellery course at Art School, Gwen built what they grandly called 'the studio' in the garden. It was, in reality, an insulated wooden shed with a bathroom, but it did the job and served as Ariana's first workshop until she started her gallery in a converted chapel in the middle of Freshwater Bay.

"Put that *bloomin'* phone down, while you're at the table," Gwen told her off.

She wanted a proper conversation with her granddaughter but all she seemed to be doing recently was staring at her phone.

Ariana put it in her pocket. Still no word from Luc. It was now five weeks, six days and two hours, but who was counting? She glanced at the ring on her hand. His ring hadn't come back by post. She hoped he'd got it.

"Who you hoping to hear from?" Gwen probed.

"No one," she answered cagily.

"Hmm. Don't give me that, Ariana. I know you. You've not told me about a boyfriend in ages. You got a new man in your life?"

"*Gwen!*"

"I'm not being funny, right, but *I've* got a better sex life than you these days, my girl," Gwen shrugged as Ariana's mouth dropped wide open.

"What with *Ed the Dead*!"

"Don't call him that. Not to his face anyway." Gwen laughed, " That name'll stick."

Gwen cleared their empty plates into the sink.

"Ellen says her Madog's single again," she floated, hoping to plant the seed.

She filled the sink with water to wash the dishes.

"Ta, Gwen. But I'm not having you and Ellen trying to fix me up, alright? Anyway y'know how I feel about those Morgan boys," Ariana replied frankly, grabbing a tea towel to help her

"Rhys is a lovely boy."

"*Hmph.*"

Conversation closed. If only Gwen knew about Mr Charming's antics.

Never mind the drugs, Ariana could never forgive him because she'd wanted him to be her first and he wasn't. Instead, she'd found Adam Williams, Rhys' idiot friend, a couple of weeks later. After the prom night, she went on a mission to rid herself of the V card and Adam had willingly obliged, *doing* her, drunk, up against a wall, behind the bins of a town bar. *Ugh!* She wasn't proud of that five-minute episode, but that *was* all Rhys' fault too. If he'd have treated her properly she'd never, ever have done that. She remembered feeling sore, straightening her miniskirt, looking at the used condom on the ground and thinking that sex was *definitely* overhyped.

Why was she even thinking about those losers again? She shook her head to dismiss them from her mind. Even ten years down the line, she still felt raw about it all. But in spite of herself, she could never forget Rhys' almost turquoise blue eyes. She hated to admit it to herself, but when she visualised Luc, she saw Rhys. Which was *very* bad. And the reason why she was terrified about ever meeting Luc. She knew it would be a huge disappointment, like every other man in her life had been since him.

The Welsh March weather was as crappy as Rhys remembered it to be. The wind was icy and the rain outside the station was driving down in sheets, bouncing off the pavement and forming deep puddles on the kerbside. The wind, the mud, the driving rain. It's great to be back home, he thought bitterly as he buried himself deeper into his light jacket, pulling his lapels up higher as he walked through the ticket barrier. He wasn't used to this freezing cold and now he was about to get soaking wet too.

He'd taken his ring off as the train approached the station and it was now stowed safely in his pocket. Too many people were familiar with Ariana's work in this place.

He saw Gareth waiting for him at the station entrance, holding a spare padded waterproof coat.

"Thought you might need one of these," his eldest brother suggested thoughtfully. "Welcome home, Rhys. Great to see you, man."

It was *so* good to see Gareth again too. Rhys gave him a strong bear hug that surprised them both. And then coats on, they rushed through the pouring rain over to the car park.

"Country boy now then?" Rhys joshed as he saw Gareth's muddy builder's truck.

"Yip. Best damn thing I ever did moving back home."

He certainly looked well; Rhys agreed.

Gareth gripped his shoulder.

"Have you told them yet?"

How was he going to face his parents? It would be a surprise when they saw he'd come home. Ellen would be disappointed, he knew, but he had to face them sooner rather than later. He'd been in the air for twelve hours and then on trains for seven. He was seriously jetlagged. He needed a little bit of recovery time first.

"No," Rhys shrugged.

Gareth took Rhys' bags and popped them into the back of the pickup. His brother was looking thin. Probably some Hollywood gluten-free, macrobiotic diet he was on. He'd have to get Beth to ask him about that. She'd relish that challenge.

"Don't worry. You can stay with us at the boathouse for as long as you want. It will buy you some peace and quiet tonight. But once the word gets out, you'd better go see Mam or there'll be Hell to pay."

"Fair enough," Rhys answered, his mouth curving into a grin.

"Congratulations, by the way. I'm looking forward to meeting Beth. How did you two meet again?"

"Now, there's a story," Gareth chuckled and reversed his truck out of the station car park.

"The baby's due in a couple of weeks or so. Actually, you'll be doing us a favour by staying. We could really do with your help if you're free."

"No probs. I'm taking a bit of time out to...err... re-centre."

"I hate to ask... but can you give us a hand on the bar? The barman's quit last week and we could do with a *resting* movie star to help shift cocktails."

"Sure. No worries."

Rhys grimaced at the irony of putting a recovering alcoholic to work on the bar. How was this going to pan out? Could he resist the temptation every night? He'd worked bars fine in the past. He would *bloody well* try now.

"So... tell me, then, about these A-lister Hollywood girlfriends of yours?"

34

Gareth turned to give him a cheeky smile but saw that Rhys was out like a light. The jet lag must have kicked in already he thought.

Rhys closed his eyes and pretended to be asleep as the truck rattled the twenty miles back to Freshwater Bay. No more lies, he told himself.

Rhys liked Beth from the get-go. She was ballsy and beautiful, funny and sharp. Perfect for Gareth. And it made Rhys feel even more alone. She'd made him his favourite dish, a fish pie. It was a triumph of texture with a firm crunchy Panko topping and a silky, creamy sauce around the fish and seafood pieces. The sophistication was swanky restaurant, the taste was all home.

They sat around the table in the boathouse chatting.

"Wine?"

Rhys covered his glass with his hand as Gareth went to pour him a cold, crisp white.

"Not for me. Don't drink anymore."

"Hollywood diet eh?"

Rhys let it pass. He wasn't up to telling them yet.

Beth gushed, "I was so nervous cooking for a Hollywood superstar. I still can't believe you're eating dinner with us."

Rhys winced.

"Tell us *all* about it. Who've you filmed with recently?"

"I haven't worked in a while," answered politely.

"Do you ever get to go to Hollywood parties?"

"No."

What's it like to live out at the beach?"

"I wouldn't know."

He sipped his water; he didn't mean to sound churlish. He tried to make amends.

"This is honestly the best fish pie I've ever tasted. You're some chef, Beth, you know that? Is that truffle oil I can taste going in there?"

Beth nodded and gave him a quirky smile.

"How are you enjoying living here after years in London?" he asked, deflecting the conversation successfully.

They chatted, but it was clear to Beth that Rhys was running away from something.

Gareth was surprised too, as he was usually full of big stories. His brother sounded flat. He held Beth's hand under the table and gave it a squeeze. His mother was always rattling off the A-listers Rhys was hanging with, talking about him as if he already had a star on Hollywood's Walk of Fame. Why did he not want to talk about it, he wondered?

After the meal, the jetlag was starting to bite hard for real. Rhys helped Gareth to clear up while Beth went to rest.

"Just to let you know, if you ever knock me up again, Gareth Morgan, I will kill you," she complained as she hauled herself up towards the stairs to bed.

"*Aw*, cariad. I was hoping for a rugby team," he quipped with a grin.

"How many's that?" she replied, turning to Rhys.

"Fifteen plus reserves."

"That's it. I'm booking you in as soon as we're done here."

Her fingers made a pair of scissors at Gareth, and Rhys sniggered as his brother reddened.

She was tiny and that bump was huge. Rhys winced, that had to hurt when it came out. Women, how could they do that? And his brother Gareth, *about to become a dad!* It wasn't that long since he was divorced and sworn off women for life. Things changed fast. He just hoped that one day he'd find someone and be as happy and in love as they obviously were.

The men went outside after clearing up and stood, drinking tea on the deck of the boathouse looking out at the sea. It had stopped raining, but the night was black, and it was still breezy.

"So glad you're back, Rhys. It's not been the same with you gone." Gareth gripped his brother's arm.

Rhys nodded to his brother; he had missed him too.

"This place is seriously cool."

Gareth had moved there when Beth first arrived. It had been a large, wooden shed with a slipway down to the sea. Gareth had stripped it back and turned it into a Scandinavian style cabin with a large living space and wall to wall windows opening out to a deck and the sea.

Gareth knew Rhys would like it.

"So modern and light. You're a genius, man. Remember when we used to play in here?" Rhys reminisced.

"I remember you used to come here to smoke dope with your dodgy mates."

Rhys smirked.

"How did you know?" Rhys asked.

"Smelled like Bob Marley's living room, pal. Thankfully, Dad never cottoned on. Keeps telling me though how he used to like the sweet smell of the boathouse."

They laughed. His traditional parents had never coped with Rhys' wildness.

"Well, you've certainly hit the jackpot on this place, and on Beth. You're a lucky man, Gareth Morgan."

"That I am." Gareth agreed. Not that it had been plain sailing.

"Thanks for putting me up. Saved me from staying at the farm."

They shared a knowing look. Gareth knew what Rhys meant by that. His parents meant well, but it could be suffocating staying there. Especially when his mother decided to play matchmaker and invite every eligible young woman in the village over for tea. They also had Madog and Jake living in one wing of the farm, so they had a house full. Madog was the youngest brother, a single dad for Jake, his two-year-old boy.

"Glad to have you here. Just no dope, yeah?"

"No drugs, no booze. I'm a changed man."

The spare room was comfortable enough for a few nights. Beth had made up the sofa bed and the computer and boxes of papers and files were piled up on a desk in one corner. Rhys could see that he'd taken up space they needed. Presumably, this would be the nursery once the baby was a little older. Gareth would need to design an extension soon, especially if he got his way and they were working on breeding a rugby team.

He lay back on the sofa bed, his long legs poking out of the bottom. This is what his career had come to, kipping on a-put-you-up bed at his brother's place. He grateful to them for this stopgap but he'd have to find somewhere more permanent soon. He just hoped that he wouldn't have to move back to the farm.

CHAPTER FIVE

He'd been back in the country for twenty-four hours. He knew he'd have to go over to see his parents today. Any longer and he'd be off their Christmas list for good, he laughed silently to himself. But his anxiety was back, and he was prevaricating. His throat was dry, and his heart rate was raised. He knew he had to get this over and done with. It was stressing him out and that stress was giving him the overwhelming urge to drink.

He'd had strong temptations before, but this was taking over his mind. His head was cajoling him, chipping away his resolve, grinding his defences down. What he really needed was a little Dutch courage to get him through. A couple of small shots and he wouldn't care. He scoured the kitchen units in the boathouse. Nothing. An opened bottle of white wine and a couple of beers in the fridge. No spirits, thank God. The demon was screaming for him to down the wine.

"Owen, I need help."

Rhys was sweating as his hand was stuck on the fridge door like a magnet, the other on his phone.

"I don't think I can do this."

"Where are you?" Owen talked to him down the phone.

"At the boathouse. I've got to go to the farm and face Mam. There's a bottle of wine in the fridge. I'm going to down it."

Owen read the situation. He needed to get him away from the temptation.

"What you wearing?"

"Eh?"

"What you wearing? Go and get your running kit on now."

Rhys did as he was told without questioning Owen.

"Right. Come with me. Keep me by you. Get out of the boathouse now and jog up the track. You can do this Rhys, it's nearly two months. You're literally home and dry."

Rhys ran up the hill, with his ear to the phone until he was at the top of the gravelly lane. He paused, out of breath as he reached the car park to La Galloise. He was out of danger.

"What would I do without you, man?" Rhys' voice became thick, not just from running.

"What would I do without you? Now get your butt over to Mam's and suck it up. What's the worst she can do? Anytime you feel like that again, you stick those running shoes on, *yeah*, and get the Hell out of there."

"'Kay, thanks, bro."

How did Owen get so wise, Rhys wondered? He was right. The trigger was fear. He had to face things. He jogged down the hill through Freshwater Bay and up the lane towards the farm. Spring was just popping out the hedgerows. Tiny green buds were forming on the dark hawthorn spikes giving just a hint of warmer times ahead.

He braced himself as he reached the farm, patted the dogs who came out to meet him, and mustering up an award-winning performance, he casually breezed into the kitchen as if he'd never been away.

Ellen, his mother, squawked in shock when she saw him and showered him with mother hen kisses, smothering him in a tight embrace.

"David," she shrieked. "Get down here. It's Rhys. He's home."

David came in from the study where he'd been paying bills and gave his son a warm, long embrace.

"Welcome home. Good to have you back, son."

Rhys exhaled deeply and nodded at his father.

"Why didn't *anyone tell me* you were coming home?" Ellen grumbled as she moved between getting lunch ready and fussing over her son.

Rhys sat at the kitchen table and listened to her patiently.

"And *why on Earth* are you staying at the boathouse, not here?" she asked, put out.

"*Uhh*," Rhys replied, prevaricating, "Gareth needed someone around with the baby due any day, and I said I'd give Beth a hand on the bar."

"Mmm," Ellen groused, did he really hate farm work that much?

By this time, Jake had made an appearance. He'd been with his granddad in the office while Madog was on the tractor. Jake gave Rhys a welcome distraction. He was always so good with children, Ellen thought, as she watched him play with Jake.

True to form, Ellen's questions started ramping up through lunch. This is what he'd been dreading. The interrogation. She wanted *all* the details. Every show, every part, every name drop. Rhys swore if she could, she'd be taking notes. No doubt to get the bragging rights on everything he did.

What had started off as a bit of fun at his mother's expense was now a complex web of lies. It pained him to see how far away from reality his fantasy life was. But now it had to stop. It was part of the promise he had made to himself, part of his recovery plan.

He told her flat, "I'm done with Hollywood. I want a new start. Here. Maybe go back into theatre."

Rhys saw Ellen's face drop.

"But you loved doing TV and movies?"

"No. *You* did."

Rhys looked at her pointedly. Plenty of other actors didn't have the family support he'd had. She'd taken him everywhere as a kid. She'd been like his agent. But he often wondered whose dream it had been. His or hers?

She rattled on and on through lunch, asking more and more questions. He'd given up halfway through, breaking his promise to himself and telling her two whoppers.

Yes, he'd sold the condo in Santa Monica. *Bollocks!* Lie number one. *He never had one.* He'd made that up a while ago when he told her he was living out at the beach. He couldn't tell her the truth that he rented a suffocatingly hot, tiny apartment above a butcher's in San Pedro. The dockside views weren't quite up there with the sable coloured sands of Venice Beach.

That was swiftly followed by whopper number two. *Yes*, his agent would still be able to call him if a big part came up. The agent had given up on him about six months ago *when he'd turned up on set late again and still drunk.*

David sat and watched it all play out, studying Rhys, saying nothing. He picked up Jake, who was now playing with a toy tractor.

"Let's show your Uncle Rhys some real tractors."

David had thrown him a lifeline. Rhys smiled gratefully at his dad and they went outside to walk around the sheds with Jake, away from Ellen. Rhys liked walking with his father. He was always so quiet and considered. When David spoke, people listened carefully.

They walked through the lambing shed. Rhys still didn't feel any different about farming. Driving the tractor bored him stupid and he'd always resented the daily chores, feeding the calves, getting up to do the milking at silly o'clock before school. It was only the lambs he liked. So fragile, they braved the cold March weather they were born into, to keep going and grow strong. A metaphor for his recovery, he hoped.

He crouched down beside Jake.

"Look," he said, pointing to the lambs in the next field.

"See the lambs lining up over there. They're having a race."

A gang of ten lambs shot off across the field, sprinting off in a line like a school sports day.

Jake giggled as one lamb jumped high with all four legs kicking out like a snowboarder getting air.

"Meh mehs, jumping," Jake squealed.

"Yeah, buddy. Can *you* do that?" Rhys answered and chuckled at Jake trying to prance like a lamb. They leaned on a gate and watched the lambs in the field some more.

"Thanks Dad for getting me out of there."

"She means well, you know."

He didn't make eye contact with his son. Both men looked out on the field, leaning up against the gate, with Jake now sat on the top rail held safe in Rhys' strong arms.

"Yeah, I know. But I'm done with Hollywood. I don't want to talk about it. It just didn't work out for me."

Rhys knew David wouldn't push him. When he was ready he would tell him about it. Just not yet.

"I'll talk to her. Son, whatever it is, take some time and figure it out here. With your family."

"Thanks, Dad."

Rhys put Jake carefully back on the ground and hugged David tight, blinking away the tears that were stinging in his eyes. He'd never done so much hugging. It felt good.

"Hi. I'm Rhys, I've been sober for 50 days. Had a bit of a wobble today, but made it through, to hopefully get to day 51."

The circle of people smiled and said hello back to him. He'd found an AA group in town and had gone there after the farm, borrowing Beth's ancient little shopper car. It would be a breeze after facing down his mother over lunch, he told himself, trying to find the nerve to open the door and walk into the meeting. What if they were all hardened alcoholics falling off their chairs? They weren't. What if he knew someone there? Thankfully, he didn't.

When he met the group, it turned out they were all surprisingly normal, which showed you what a sneaky disease alcoholism was. It snuck up on you when you were at your lowest and gave you the false comfort blanket of an addiction. He didn't say much but knew he could come here again. Before working on the bar. Owen had really saved his ass today but having other recovering friends around him would help him too, over time. They walked in *his* shoes every day.

The next morning, Beth showed him around La Galloise. Rhys had worked in restaurants and bars all his life and he could tell straight away that Beth wasn't some amateur. She had taken the place to a whole new level and he liked what she was doing, *a lot*. The real ales were craft and artisan. The cocktails were played up for drama. They used a bit too much dry ice for his taste but *hey*, it was her show. He gave her a smirk when she asked him what he could do.

He made an L.A. Slingshot for her with gin, cherry vodka and grenadine, topped with soda.

"You like it?" he said, eager to please.

Beth smiled at him as she took a small sip to taste. How did he know cherry drinks were her favourite?

"Hey Paul, come try this."

Beth called her deputy chef over.

Paul shook hands with Rhys as Beth introduced them. Rhys studied him carefully. The faded military tattoos on his rich brown skin, his uniform immaculately pressed, shiny boots. Paul took a drink and tasted it carefully.

"I like it. There's a kick to it but it's not overpowering, and you've got a nice balance of cherry and pomegranate going on," he said impressed. His rich, deep voice had an air of authority.

They started talking food and cocktails pairings. Paul liked Rhys well enough, but he couldn't help but worry about him. There was something about him, buried behind his smile, his eyes were closed off and distant. It reminded him of some of the kids he was with in Afghanistan. The ones that were trying to keep going to get through. He checked himself. He wasn't going to mention that to Beth. He was Gareth's brother, it was best not to raise any concerns, but rather to watch him and see how he got on.

Beth didn't pry as to why he didn't drink. It was probably a sensible lifestyle choice for a barman. And he'd obviously had heaps of experience working a bar and making cocktails.

"You know, with a palate like yours, Paul and I could train you to be a chef. It's the balance and flavours that most people struggle with," she suggested.

Rhys thought about it.

"I'm not sure that's for me," he reflected honestly.

Paul made his excuses and left. He had a gooseberry and apple chutney that he was making which needed checking and stirring.

"You're a natural," she grinned at him, chipping away.

"Gareth can't even boil water, but don't tell him I said so."

The baby kicked. Rhys noticed it and was staring in wonder at her huge bump which was clearly moving underneath her shirt. Beth was suddenly self-conscious. There was no way she could stretch any further, this baby *had* to come out soon.

"You can feel it move if you like. But, I warn you, it's weird."

She laughed as Rhys put his hand out towards her and she placed it gently on her stomach just as an elbow *or was it a foot*, came jutting powerfully out.

He gasped.

"You laugh. There's a full soccer match going on in there."

Rhys took Beth's hand.

"I'm so pleased for you both."

"Yeah me too. It took us a while, but we finally got there."

Rhys agreed to work evening shifts for her. It was simple enough, he told himself. Just serve the drinks and keep away from tasting any. It was a test. And he knew he could do it. The afternoon shift was wrapping up and that evening Rhys took over his first shift from Courtney, a cool looking hipster who was off to try and catch a couple of waves before dusk. She dropped him a flirty smile and his lips curved into a cheeky grin back. She wasn't his type, but it lifted his mood; right up until he saw who was standing there staring at him. *Ariana.* Apparently, she was managing the floor this shift and looked just as shocked as he was, when she saw him; flirting. *Way to go, Rhys.*

She looked even more beautiful than he remembered. Dressed in the uniform, like him, of a navy sailor-striped top. She wore black trousers and a short apron round her waist. Her long, dark hair was tied up in a high ponytail, accenting her almond-shaped eyes and olive skin. Why hadn't Gareth *told* him that she worked here?

"Ari."

Her heart jumped. No one called her Ari. Except him.

"Okay, *Tom Cruise*," she addressed him prissily, "Let's get going. Three pints of Moretti and a Pornstar Martini for table four."

She put down the check and his eyes were immediately drawn to her hand. She was wearing a matching ring to the one she'd sent him. His chest pounded. He'd think about that later. Here, now, she was all business with him. Cold even. He gave her his best smile in acknowledgement and started pouring the first pint into a frozen glass. She turned, and as the beer flowed, he watched her walk away. God, he loved her ass in those trousers. It proved a great distraction as he made a perfect cocktail. When she came back to collect the drinks, she scrutinised them, reluctantly impressed.

"Not bad."

A couple of locals sat at the bar, drinking pints of ale. Tommy Shop, the store owner, and John the Catch, the local fisherman, had moved their custom from the Lobster Pot to La Galloise and were now regular fixtures at the bar.

"They clean their beer lines up here," Tommy told Rhys under his breath.

Things at the Lobster Pot did not sound good. Apparently, it was pretty dead there, even at weekends. John and Tommy snickered as they noticed Ariana loading Rhys with checks all night, not speaking except to curtly give him drink orders, her face stony, not cracking, despite his best efforts.

"Don't know what you've done to get Ariana so pissy," John ribbed Rhys.

Rhys threw them a quizzical look. It was ten years, and he still wasn't forgiven, he could tell. The bar was busy, but he handled it in his stride. Much to Ariana's annoyance.

As the night went on and the service wrapped up, Ariana sent the junior waiting-on staff home. But the barman was always the last to leave, serving until last orders at eleven. She had to stay too. It was getting a little awkward as the place was getting quieter and the customers were leaving. She felt him staring at her.

Rhys brought up so many emotions. There was the visceral hate, but she knew *that* was a protection mechanism to help her when her heart thumped at the very sight of him. She'd acted professionally all evening. Given him the orders. Refused to react to that *damn* disarming smile of his. She could almost see the cartoon sparkling stars twinkle at the side of his whitened teeth. And those same blue eyes, like the summer sea. He certainly looked buff. L.A. obviously suited him well. Why was he here though, working the bar? *No way* was she asking. And *how* was she going to cope with this every evening? She couldn't let Beth down and she badly needed the money. Why was *she* even thinking like this? *He* was the one who'd come here, disturbed her world, made her feel so... so... *unsettled.*

"I'll finish off on the bar, you can go now," she told him directly.

"It's no bother to wait," he answered nonchalantly.

"No. You go."

She dismissed him.

That was that. Grabbing his coat, he set out in the driving rain, down the muddy track back to the boathouse.

Bianca: Luc? Are you there? I REALLY need to talk

It was past midnight. He was on his laptop sitting up in the sofa bed, trying to unwind. He had his headphones on and was trying to watch a film, playing distractedly with the Claddagh ring in his hand, his mind drifting to Ariana. Gareth and Beth were upstairs, and although Gareth had done a great job on the renovations, the sound still carried.

Bianca: Luc? It says you're online. You there?

What should he do? He'd been determined to close their chat forever. He'd shut down the Celtic Art website when he'd gone to rehab. Exit stage left. But she'd been wearing that ring; he knew how invested she was in Luc. She obviously loved Luc and still hated Rhys. So, he reasoned, why couldn't he slip back into character for a while, *right*?

He looked down at that beautiful ring, now warm in his hand and slipped it onto his finger. What harm could it do to answer? Luc was thousands of miles away, in her head. He started typing.

Luc: Hey Bianca. Wassup?

Bianca: You're back? From rehab?

Luc: Yeah nearly two months sober and counting... every freakin' minute

45

Bianca: I'm so proud of you

Luc: Yeah. Me too. I got your ring. It's awesome. I've never seen anything like it. Thank you. It kept me strong

Bianca: Sending you Celtic powers. Trust, faith and friendship

He noticed she didn't mention the Celtic love knot she'd put on it.

Bianca: How you feeling these days? Is life better for you?

Luc: Making some big life changes at the moment, and you know, I'm feeling more positive. Nothing feels black now

Bianca: Luc, I care about you so much, I just want you to be happy and well

Luc: Me too. It still hurts and I get anxious but I'm trying to face my fears

Bianca: I know what you mean

Luc: Why? What's bugging you?

Bianca: My ex. Rhys. He's back home and working in the restaurant with me

He gave her a Greg question.

Luc: How do you feel about that?

Bianca: I hate him. I'm soooo confused

Brutal. Say it like you mean it, why don't you, Ariana.

Luc: When did you split?

Bianca: Years ago, in high school. We were eighteen. He tried to make a secret sex video of us on Prom night

Luc: Jerk!

Bianca: Yeah. Getting me into a hotel room without asking first was bad enough. I was scared, I'd never done it before

He thought she'd been winding him up. No wonder she'd run.

Luc: Did he know?

Bianca: He never bothered to ask. He was a total wanker

He didn't disagree. He'd never deserved her.

Luc: So... why are you confused?

Ariana paused. How could she talk to Luc about how her stomach had been churning every time she looked over to the bar? How, when he was serving a customer, her eyes had traced the shape of his muscular pectorals through his T-shirt uniform that was a little too tight for him.

Bianca: You're so right, I'm not confused. Ok, so I am still. Argghhhhh!!!!

Luc: You know, Bianca. It was a long time ago. He sounds like a young, arrogant jackass who was out to impress the guys. I'm sure he's changed and would feel real bad about it now

Bianca: WTF! Defending the guy corner?

Luc: No. Just think it's a long time since high school. You so should talk to him

Bianca: Not sure I can get the words out when I see him. He makes me... flustered

Interesting. He thought she was cold and off with him. She didn't look like the tongue-tied type.

Luc: You need to talk to him. It'll help you work out that anger at least?

It'd give him a chance to apologise, properly. And hopefully, she'd forgive him.

Bianca: Yeah, I s'pose. Thanks, Luc. God, I love chatting to you. Please don't stop

He was a total shit and he'd just done it again. Deceived the girl he loved.

Luc: OK.

Bianca: Promise me one more thing

Luc: Yes?

Bianca: No more bridges?

Luc: I promise, Bianca. No more bridges. I chose life, remember

Bianca: Yes. Thank God! When can I come see you?

Luc: Not yet.

Rhys shut the laptop and rubbed his eyes. What had he done? He was back in deep again as Luc.

CHAPTER SIX

Ariana was doing her least favourite thing. She was staring at the spreadsheet in front of her. The outgoings were stacking up. Electricity, water, materials, oil to heat the gallery. It was frightening how quickly the money was draining out of her account. The reality of the situation screamed at her. She needed to do more sales *and fast* or she'd be out of business in a few weeks. She didn't need the analytics on her website to tell her that her hits were worryingly low, she hadn't made a sale since Valentine's Day, over a month ago. And the money from the extra shifts at La Galloise wouldn't begin to cover her outgoings.

She rubbed her eyes and looked away from the screen. What was she doing wrong? Her gallery, the converted chapel, was full of interesting and eclectic pieces. Other local artists were relying on her to help find them sales too. She took a cut in the final price. It worked as a business model, but the whole thing had been boosted by the American sales which had now dried up. She needed to talk to Luc, see if he could get his site back up and running again. *Stuff his issues,* she thought, she needed him now to help her out of this tough patch.

The large oak chapel door squeaked open and Ariana turned to see who was coming in.

"Hey, Ari."

Shit! It was Rhys.

He wandered into the gallery a little nervously.

"Alright? How's it going? Cool place you got here."

Lame, he thought. What was he doing? Why had he convinced himself to come here? He'd not seen her since the shift two nights ago and he'd run out of patience waiting to see her. After the conversation he had with her online as Luc, he had taken a fit and decided it was up to him to get the ball rolling and visit her at the gallery. Judging by the look of horror on her face now, it wasn't one of his best ideas. Rhys gazed around, trying to defuse the tension that had built up in the space between them. He nodded at the large chandelier of coloured glass shards hanging from the ceiling,

"Are these all your pieces?"

Ariana didn't speak for a moment. How was she going to play this? She rubbed her face with her hands, trying to ease the pulse in her temples and got up from the computer on her desk.

"*Err...* no, they're from local artists. I showcase them here and try to help get them sold. *In theory.*"

Her voice dried up and Rhys heard it crack.

"What you doing here, Rhys?"

Rhys ignored her. He was studying a collection of abstract paintings, very modern, the colours maybe a little muted for Californian tastes, but these moody seascapes would sell well, he was sure. She just needed to get them out there more. It was about the hits and the visibility. He walked around, studying the pieces. Ariana had excellent taste. It was a coherent collection and every individual item felt fresh. "Where's *your* stuff?"

Ariana's eyes widened. What did he want, she wondered?

"Over here."

She led him to the Celtic jewellery pieces she'd designed and created. Rhys knew them all too well. He loved what she was doing with her jewellery, taking the boho vibe of stacked bangles and necklaces, and interweaving them with intricate Celtic art. He looked at a Celtic cross sitting in a layered necklace. Just like Ariana. Very cool.

Even in work dungarees, hair tied up with a scarf, she looked stunning. Not like Hollywood stunning, where everyone was tanned, lip pumped, botoxed and coiffured. Ariana had her own style and a big part of it was that she didn't realise just how beautiful she was. He loved that about her. He turned to her, standing a little too closely for Ariana's liking. She started to shuffle backwards.

"Ari, I've come to say sorry."

She blinked and stared at him, a little shocked.

"You know," he hedged nervously, "We... we're obviously going to be working together at the restaurant, and I don't want things to be *weird* between us."

Rhys coughed. She was making him work hard.

"It was a long time ago," she said, brushing him off, looking down at her boots.

"Yeah, well. I was an arrogant idiot and you were right to put me in my place. I deserved it... Friends?"

He held out his hand to her. She looked up, and then at his hand, considered his offer and then, reluctantly, shook it. He'd made the effort to see her and he had obviously thought through what he'd done and regretted it, she reasoned. They needed to get over this if they were going to be working at the restaurant. She still didn't trust him though.

"Your work's amazing, Ari."

He hadn't let go of her hand. He held it and studied the ring on her right finger carefully.

"I really like this."

Ariana dismissed it.

"It's nothing, just a Celtic design I did."

"A Claddagh ring with the Welsh knot symbol. Heart pointing towards you. Loyalty, friendship and a pledge of love."

Ariana's eyes widened like a cat's. *How the Hell?* She looked at him suspiciously. How did he know about Celtic symbols? And why was he grinning at her with that boyish smile of his that gave her butterflies?

"Powerful stuff. Who's the lucky man?"

She flushed. *Dammit.* He was doing it again to her. Getting her tongue-tied and flustered.

"No one. And it's none of your business, Rhys Morgan," she snapped. "Now if you'll excuse me, I'm trying to run a business here."

She walked back to her desk and sat down by her computer.

He'd riled her. He switched tactics.

"Show me what you're doing."

He followed her and stood over her shoulder looking at the computer.

"Why?"

"Cos I'm bored."

Ariana exhaled. She gave up. Maybe some brutal honesty would help him to go away and leave her alone.

"Well, if you wanna know, I'm trying to work out how not to go out of business. I'm not shifting the pieces quickly enough and I don't think I can tough it out 'til the tourist season starts in May. I had an American buyer but that's dried up."

"Let me help you," he said gently.

"What?"

She turned and looked at him.

"Let me help."

It was the first genuine smile she'd seen Rhys give her, and it cracked her heart open.

"Why'd you care?" she asked, genuinely puzzled.

50

"I wanna help. Make up for my previous bad behaviour," he offered persuasively.

She gazed into his eyes. What could she do when he looked at her so disarmingly like that?

"I can't afford to pay you," she told him truthfully.

"No need. It'll give me something to do in the day. You'll be doing me a favour. If I'm not busy, Dad'll be roping me into lambing... And y'know how much *I hate* farm work."

Ariana exhaled, letting out a small sigh as Rhys knocked down all the reasons why she shouldn't say yes.

"What can you do?"

"I can look at your website and sort out your online shopping points for a start. Hopefully, get you some sales. I can do more than just shake a cocktail, Ari," he shrugged and then gave her a wolfish grin, "Give me a chance, let me show you what I can do."

She wasn't an expert on this, and he was offering her free help. What did she have to lose? But what did it mean? Would she be obligated to him?

"Okay," she finally relented, deflated.

"Great. Let's see this website of yours."

Rhys hadn't felt this good in a long time. Ariana was giving him a chance, and he was determined to prove to her what he could do.

Ariana showed Rhys her websites and her online presence, writing down usernames and passwords. They were pretty basic. But Rhys already knew that. He could sort this out and bring back Luc to help if it meant she was going to go out of business. He hadn't realised how much the US sales had boosted her business and the effect that freezing his site had had on her. He could easily restart it again, get Luc to suggest to her shipping the stuff from Wales direct. It would give him time to build her a better site and link her into online shopping over in the UK and in The States. He got to work.

Three hours later, a loud whoop sounded from the workshop. Rhys looked up from behind the desk where he was working on Ariana's computer.

"Hey, Rhys! I've just sold the seascape mural on the back wall," she called from the workshop, coming through to see him, her phone in her hand as proof.

51

Rhys looked over to her and grinned. It retailed at twelve hundred pounds and she'd made twenty per cent on the sale.

"Well done, Ariana."

They were talking like old friends now.

"It was sold on an online art store. Did you post it up?" she asked.

She rushed up and leaned over him as he showed her what he'd done. She smelled *so* good and he could feel her hastened breathing. She was suddenly unsteady around him, nervous even. It was all he could do to stop himself turning to her, there and then, and kissing her, but he knew she'd be spooked, and he'd be out the door, probably with a slapped face. He needed to work to gain her trust first. He cleared his throat as he attempted to clear those thoughts away.

He croaked, "Yeah. I've linked different pieces to different places. Places where I think they'll sell."

Ariana looked at what Rhys had done.

"The sites get a small cut too. But it'll help shift the pieces. You may need to put the prices up a little to accommodate the extra commission."

"Wow! You've done this in a couple of hours. I'm impressed."

Rhys had not only linked her pieces to online marketplaces, fashion and art stores, but had also started to rebuild her website. He needed to take some better photos of the pieces and then revamp the look of her WordPress site.

"I'll need to bring my camera down and take more shots of the pieces tomorrow."

"Thank you."

She smiled sweetly at him and it was now his heart's turn to skip a beat.

"There's still a lot to do. But hopefully, it will generate more sales for you."

Ariana was grateful to him for the help. She'd secretly enjoyed having Rhys around in the gallery through the morning and it would make it easier when they were working in the restaurant. Hopefully, it would also help her to get over feeling like a schoolgirl, every time he looked at her. Was there still something between them? She felt it when she'd leaned over. She definitely felt a tension, an electricity between them. Or was it just her projecting? The last thing she needed to do now was to get a crush on Rhys Morgan. The man she'd hated for so long.

Mid-afternoon, Rhys left abruptly. He was off to town for something before the evening shift. Ariana watched him go as she wrapped up the seascape piece to post. This wasn't the Rhys she knew. As a kid he could never sit still for more than five minutes, never mind five hours. And in the short time that day, he'd done more than she could have done in a month. But he was an actor. Where had he learned those web skills, she wondered? And what was the catch? How long would he stick it until he got bored? Who cared. She'd made two more sales and a whack of commission that afternoon. She needed to thank him, not question his motives.

She should have apologised too. *She* had posted that picture of him all those years ago, and he'd had to live that down in front of all his mates for months. She'd be in big trouble if she'd have done it now. There were laws these days on revenge porn.

And he'd been mercilessly teased about it. He'd been called 'Rhys the Cock' all summer. The rugby team had even made a Rhys pinata, essentially a huge cock and balls, and put it above the clubhouse bar, where it sat for two years until it got smacked down in a brawl. She'd shamed him publicly. Probably not a good thing for an actor. What could she do? He said he didn't want paying for his work. Maybe she could get him an expensive bottle of Napa wine? To remind him of California. Beth had a bottle in stock on the menu that she could buy from her before the shift at a wholesale price. They were both working that evening; it would be perfect timing.

"Come down to the Lobster Pot when you get off work."

Courtney the other bar worker was wangling for a hook-up with Rhys. Rhys had just come onto the shift with Dan, who was waiting on tables. And Courtney practically jumped him as soon as he walked through the door, Dan noted in admiration. He then watched on as Courtney leaned in towards Rhys with doe eyes, just as Ariana, Miss Cool herself, came up to the bar, gift bag in hand, for him. Another one of his many admirers. How does he do it, Dan meditated in awe? The man was *a legend.*

Ariana immediately regretted taking over the bottle of wine. Rhys was standing there with Courtney, who was clearly flirting with him. To be fair to Rhys, he hadn't even taken his coat off when she'd pounced. There was something about that girl that Ariana didn't like.

"I'll see how it goes," Ariana heard him replying to Courtney.

"Great. See you later then."

Courtney threw Ariana a triumphant look as she pulled her apron off, stuffed it into her jacket and got ready to leave. And there she was, lining up behind her, like a kid waiting to see Santa. What was she doing? Seriously. But she was there at the bar now, present in hand, and she couldn't exactly scurry away with everyone, including Rhys, looking at her. She thrust the gift bag towards him.

Rhys had no intention of seeing Courtney, but he had liked that look of disgust and outright jealousy that Ariana had given her when she left. It gave him hope that she liked him.

"Thank you for your help today. Made four sales so far." Ariana was flushed with embarrassment.

"Buzzin'."

Rhys' eyes sparkled dangerously at her.

"Yeah, you did well."

"Not finished yet, I've only made a start. What's this?"

She felt a slight thread of panic as his eyes locked hungrily on hers. He switched his attention to the gift bag she'd placed on the bar in front of him. He looked at her and opened it; then she saw his face cloud over suddenly as he stared coldly at the red wine Ariana had bought for him, wrapped in an extravagant crepe bow. What was he going to tell her? What he'd give to share that bottle with her, he dreamed; on that driftwood log, watching the sun set. It was a sore temptation, but he swept it aside.

"Thanks. You didn't need to do that. Ari, I don't drink."

"Oh God! I didn't know."

She looked put out.

He hadn't meant to be ungrateful and he tried to pacify her.

"I'm just glad to help out. No need to repay me."

"Miss! I ordered a medium steak and this one is well done."

A disgruntled looking lady from table seven was stomping towards Ariana at the bar holding a plate with a half-chewed steak, which she proceeded to push under Ariana's nose. She seemed to be enjoying drawing the attention of the other customers.

Furrowing her brow, Ariana examined the plate carefully.

"Yes. I can see it's well done. I'm very sorry. I'll get you a new one right away."

Ariana tried to mollify her and contain the complaint as other customers began to turn around and were now watching the little scene at the bar. The woman still looked indignant as she walked away and was now talking loudly about the reviews of the place and how it was not living up to her expectations.

"Ari?"

Rhys nodded her over to him and she came back to the bar.

"What they drinking? She's making a bit of a fuss. Would Beth mind if I offered her a drink?"

"Go for it," Ariana told him. Anything was better than facing that old, sour-faced, battle-axe again. She'd tried her best, but you could see that she was hanging out for a full refund, with her four lady friends in tow. Ariana went to check on the recook of the steak. It would be another ten minutes and the other ladies on the table were ploughing through their plates at full pelt.

Ariana watched as Rhys approached the table and treated the cantankerous old bag to his most dazzling smile. She melted. It was embarrassing, Ariana thought; she was twice his age. He suggested something to her quietly. And what was that, Ariana observed? A high-pitched girlish giggle. Really? Was that coming from The Old Battle-axe? And now she was touching her hair. *Ugh!* Frosty Knickers was putty in his hands.

Rhys went away and made an orange and peach schnapps cocktail. Ariana took it over to the table and she watched as from the bar Rhys gave Old Icy Pants a cheeky half salute, like an airline pilot. He'd got things back on terms, though. Sourpuss had piped down the bolshiness and when the table left, they were giggling and merry, having paid also for the full range of puddings and a full round of Rhys' special cocktail. They all laughed as they passed Rhys and he escorted them to the door, making jokes. They'd definitely be back, they told him as they put a twenty-pound tip in his hand. What nights did he work?

Tommy Shop and John the Catch took in the spectacle and followed the women out of the door on the pretext of going for a smoke. Ariana watched them all go as she wiped their table and cleared their dirty plates, laughing silently to herself. Being such a flirt had its advantages, she thought, stacking up the plates and carrying them to the kitchen just as Rhys came crashing into her as he walked back to the bar.

"*Whoa!* That was a close one," Rhys laughed as he steadied Ariana and took the plates off her to take to the kitchen.

"How did you do that back there? You have a gift," Ariana teased.

He looked at Ariana with mock shame.

"Nothing. Just offered them a little Sex on the Beach. The cocktail... Don't look at me *like that!* They *loved* it."

Ariana was now definitely scowling.

"It took her mind off the steak, *didn't it?* And I bet we get great reviews."

"Rhys Morgan you are *still* a whore-man," Ariana humphed at him and he laughed.

The restaurant and bar were quiet later on, and by ten thirty Ariana was cashing up for Beth, who had gone home early. Rhys was finishing up at the bar. If she'd overheard right, he had plans at The Lobster Pot after. He was busy emptying the slop trays and cleaning down.

She cashed up the till. Then did it again. And again. The bar takings were down by fifty pounds. It was down thirty pounds the last time Rhys had worked the shift with her. She needed to talk to Beth about it, but Beth was in no state to deal with this. It would make things super-awkward with Gareth too. She cleared her throat.

"Rhys?" she called to him.

"Yeah."

He looked up.

"The takings on the bar. They're fifty pounds down."

"You sure?"

"Err.. yeah. You've not rung through something twice or keyed in an error?"

She hoped he had.

"No. Has it happened before?"

"Mmm."

Ariana looked away.

"When?" Rhys asked.

"Your last shift. I'm not being funny, but it was down thirty quid that time too," Ariana hedged apologetically.

Rhys was angry. This was bullshit. She couldn't think he'd steal, and from his sister-in-law, could she?

"What you trying to say, Ariana? That I'm a thief? That I steal from my own family?"

"No," she said, horrified.

Hypocrite. He winced. He needed no reminding that he'd stolen from her.

"Come here. Check my pockets."

He pulled at the pocket lining on his trousers dramatically and gave her his jacket and his apron.

"Wanna strip me too? You've done that before," he growled.

She gave him an evil glare.

"I'm done here for tonight. I suggest you check that video camera before you go any further."

He threw down the towels and grabbed his jacket.

Damn. Ariana hadn't thought of that. A camera sat above the till, pointing right at her, suspiciously.

"I'm sorry, Rhys."

Her words echoed around the empty restaurant floor. He'd gone.

What the Hell had gone on back there? Rhys slumped into his bed in the boathouse guest room. Beth and Gareth were upstairs asleep, he hoped. He had fought the desire for a beer. Just a cold one after a long shift. Followed by a couple of Irish chasers to help him sleep. He opened his laptop to banish the thoughts and try to still his mind. He was still angry.

Luc: Bianca?

Ariana was back home now and online too.

Bianca: Hey. How you doing?

Luc: I've been better

Bianca: Wanna talk about it?

Luc: Not particularly

He was bouncing with Ariana and wasn't sure if he could do this right now

Bianca: It'll help

Luc: Did you talk to that guy?

Bianca: Yes. He came to see me and apologised. He helped me with my web stuff all day and then tonight I called him a thief and now he hates me

Luc: That's a pity, your website sucks. You need his help

Bianca: Gee, thanks. Kick a girl when she's down, why don't you

Luc: Why d'you call him a thief?

Bianca: The bar till was down for the second time he'd been working. He told me to check the video camera

Luc: And?

Bianca: I checked the footage. It's not Rhys. God! I feel so awful. I'm pretty sure it's Courtney. I need to show the clip to Beth but I'm sure I can see her slipping some notes into her apron when she did the changeover

Luc: Was the till ever down before Rhys started?

Bianca: The takings were down just before the last barman left. Beth assumed he'd swiped it as a parting gift. That's why she put the camera there to check

Luc: Your turn to say sorry?

Bianca: I wish. He'll never speak to me again after tonight. I wouldn't blame him. Anyway, I bought him a thank you present for today and he threw it back in my face. I can't seem to get anything right

Luc: What did you get him?

Bianca: Bottle of wine. He said he doesn't drink

Luc: Maybe he doesn't

Bianca: He used to

Luc: People change Bianca

Bianca: Maybe. Anyway, he's probably in the Lobster Pot with Courtney now. She was trying hard to get him to go

Luc: Bet he isn't

Bianca: How do you know?

Luc: Just a hunch

Bianca:?

Luc: I'm thinking of starting my website up again, but it'd save time and cost if you posted direct. What do you think?

Bianca: Yeah that'd be cool. My sales are down without your site. I'm happy to post direct if you send me the deets

Luc: OK, when I make a sale I'll forward it to you, so keep checking your emails, I'll get the site back up and running later today

Bianca: Thanks. I appreciate it

Luc: No big deal. And I'm sure he'll forgive you. Sweet dreams Bianca x

Bianca: Have a good evening, Luc x

CHAPTER SEVEN

"What you doing back here?"

It was nine am and Rhys had just walked into the gallery as if nothing had happened last night. No accusations. No recrimination. No anger. Just that *big ole smile* of his, she puzzled.

"You need the help," he said truthfully.

Trying to dampen down the feeling of relief that he was back and seemed on good terms with her, Ariana adjusted her ponytail nonchalantly as she sat at the gallery front desk.

He nearly hadn't gone in. He'd stood by the door for a full five minutes, gathering the courage to see her again. In the end, he decided he'd take a chance and go for it.

"Besides, I figured, that after you'd watched the camera footage and seen how it wasn't me, that I'd enjoy the moment when *you* apologised to *me*."

How could he be so cocky? And so *right*. *Dammit*.

"How did you know?"

"Sixth sense," he shrugged smugly. "Now for the apology?"

She stared at him as he wandered breezily up to the desk, swinging a carrier bag as he came. He was *so* milking this, she thought.

"Alright... I'm sorry." Ariana said wincing, suddenly concentrating on the computer screen. She hated backing down.

"Not going to cut it," he taunted playfully.

She looked up and met his turquoise eyes in challenge. What did she want him to do? Beg?

"Seriously?"

"No."

Her eyes narrowed. He was starting to bug her, big time.

"The deal is, I'll only help you if you let me make you breakfast."

"Breakfast?" she repeated, surprised.

"Well, we're always working evenings and days, so I figured it was as good a time as any. I've bought some things."

He held up the bag of groceries he was carrying.

"Alright," she agreed reluctantly. She hadn't eaten yet.

"Give me a minute while I shut up here. We'll walk over to mine."

They took the path over the cliffs to Gwen's house. Rhys had walked it many times; it led to one of his favourite places, a small sandy cove around the cliffs where you could swim when it was hot. Today, the sun was out but it was still cold. Ariana was wearing a woolly hat, and Rhys was wrapped in a warm scarf he'd borrowed from Gareth. After five years of Californian heat, he was still acclimatising.

"Late night in the Lobster Pot?" Ariana fished. She still wondered if he'd met up with Courtney after.

"Wouldn't know. I went home after work. I hear even the lemonade there is flat," Rhys answered breezily, smiling to himself. He was definitely in with a shot; Ariana Jones was well and truly jealous.

Her gran's cottage was just as he remembered it, and Gwen was there, feeding the chucks in the garden. She put down the bag of pellets and gave him a big hug as if she'd been expecting him.

"Hey, my favourite actor. How *are* you, cariad?"

"I'm good Mrs Jones, thank you."

"*Hisht!*" she scolded him gently. "I'm not your teacher now. Stop it with the Mrs Jones, will you, or I'll have to put you back in detention. You always *were* one of my *naughtiest* boys."

He tried again, chuckling, "*Gwen...* we're making some breakfast. You want some?"

She looked at them both.

"No, cariad. I'm just feeding these and then I'm off to yoga. Where are you staying, Rhys? At the farm?"

Her eyes were steady as she was considering something. Ariana took the grocery bag from Rhys and disappeared into the kitchen.

"*Uhh...* no. I'm with Gareth and Beth, but the baby's coming soon, so it'll be a bit crowded in the boathouse. Guess I'll be moving back in with Mam and Dad after it comes."

Gwen spotted the reluctance in his voice. She was no fool, she knew Rhys had a complicated relationship with his mother. Ellen was a good person, but she'd always lived too much through Rhys. She'd told her so too, on more than one occasion.

"Why don't you stay here?" Gwen asked him.

A plate dropped in the kitchen. Thankfully, it didn't smash. Ariana came back out into the garden and glared at Gwen.

"You could stay in the studio, Rhys. It's got a bathroom, running water, electricity, wifi. No hot tub as yet," she joked, but noted Ariana's non-verbal protests, as she desperately tried to catch her Gran's eye.

"Well, *you* won't live there," she mouthed at Ariana in reply.

60

She turned back to Rhys, "She doesn't like being on her own, prefers being in the house with me."

Ariana shook her head and gave Gwen another hard stare for making her look wimpy, but Rhys had clocked Ariana's reaction. She wasn't happy at all about this arrangement.

"No, I couldn't possibly," he told Gwen politely.

But Gwen was on a mission and there was no stopping her now.

"*Come on*. Think about it. It's a *great* idea. Ariana says you've been helping out. I know she's flat broke and can't afford to pay you. It'd be in exchange for your work in the gallery. Come and *have a look* at it at least, eh?"

Rhys went with Gwen to the studio, and Ariana shuffled behind them sulkily. What was her Gran doing? She wasn't usually a stickybeak like this.

The studio didn't look up to much at first glance, Rhys thought. And that was confirmed as he walked through the door and slammed into a large cobweb, which got firmly stuck on his face. Pulling off the sticky web, he scanned the living space. There was an ancient wood-burning stove in the corner, and in front, a dusty, stained sofa, that was plastered in the dog hairs of a long-deceased pet. Covering everything, the wooden floor and the window ledges, was a thick layer of dirty grey dust. This was more of a kennel than a cabin, he thought to himself. But, it did have running water, electricity, a toilet and a shower, albeit they hadn't seen a bottle of bleach in a good while. In the middle section of the cabin, there was an ancient paint-stained pine table with a couple of chairs by the window, but there was no bed, although there was plenty of space for one with a little rearrangement.

"We can move the spare bed out of the house and Ariana'll give you a hand to clean this place up. You can use our kitchen to eat in for now," Gwen said airily.

Rhys turned to Ariana and studied her.

"This is your place. I can't take it."

Ariana was torn and she looked away. She'd made eight sales since he'd started helping her, she reminded herself. Even though the thought of him here at the cottage made her stomach churn, she couldn't deny that she needed his help with her business. It was confusing. She *really did mean* to hate him, but he had been so *nice* to her. And, she *had* wrongly accused him of stealing. *Argghh!*

"No. It's fine," she said sulkily, beaten down.

"Gwen's right. I haven't used it in years. Stay here, if you want."

Rhys weighed it up. The place was a dump, but it gave him the ideal opportunity to spend more time with Ariana.

"The place's perfect until I get settled. Thank you, Ari."

Rhys and Ariana went back to the house and moved a double bed from the spare bedroom in the cottage into the shed, while Gwen found fresh bedding. Ariana got the vacuum cleaner out, and Rhys attacked; first the dust, and then the bathroom with cream cleaner and bleach. Filling the air with dusty motes as they cleaned, Ariana scrubbed the sofa, removing all remnants of dog. It was still pretty tatty, so she went back in the cottage and returned with a Welsh tapestry blanket to cover it. It made the space look more comfortable, she thought. It was still very basic, and there was more to do, but in an hour or so, they'd at least made the place habitable, if not yet homely.

"Bet you're starving now," Rhys guessed. He was running on empty, and Ariana didn't disagree.

"I'm going to make you a Californian breakfast. Ever had avocado and egg toast?"

"No. Sounds intriguing, though," she said, her face cracking into a smile, in spite of herself.

She watched as he made them food, feeling a little helpless about this new situation.

As he smashed the avocado, he chatted about books. Who'd have guessed, she thought, that he was a big reader? She'd been reading the American books suggested by Luc; and like Luc, Rhys' literary knowledge put her to shame. He'd probably get on well with him, she mused dreamily.

"So, what's been the favourite thing you've acted in?" she asked as she took another small bite of the delicious poached egg and avocados on the granary toast, savouring every mouthful.

"Easy. It's Shakespeare. I played Macbeth when I was in drama school. All his plays are so rich."

Ariana couldn't comment. She'd barely passed her high school exam in literature. She'd got all her information from the crib book she'd bought.

"This is *so* good," said Ariana, taking another bite.

Rhys gave her a mischievous grin.

"Well, now I'm living next door, I'm happy to make this for you any time you want."

Blushing beetroot, she looked away shyly. She still couldn't handle him close up. He was too charismatic, too powerful for her. And here he was now, sat at the table, leaning back in his chair, like it was his place and he'd been living here for years. How did *that* happen?

Back in the gallery, after breakfast, Rhys got out the camera he'd brought with him, to get the shots he needed for the online sites. Moving a display cabinet out of the way, Ariana helped him create a small photography studio area with a painted white brick wall backdrop. Rhys wanted more light on it and began trying to redirect the fixed spotlights on the beam above. Holding the ladder as he repositioned one of the spots, Ariana took in the smell of his cologne as he stretched over her. It was slightly lemony with a hint of musk. Exotic and very sexy. She pulled herself together and looked down towards the floor. She needed to stop this, now. It was Luc she wanted, she told herself, not Rhys *The Rat* Morgan. Lighting in place, Ariana hurried away to seek out an old tea box and some hessian sacking that she had in mind; it proved perfect to prop up the pieces that they needed to photograph.

By mid-afternoon, Rhys had photos of most of the smaller pieces ready to upload online and Ariana was in the back workshop putting the catch on a necklace she was finishing off.

He called through, "I'll see you later. Just off to town. Thanks again for the studio. If it's okay with you, I'll move in later, before the restaurant shift?"

He didn't have much, so it wouldn't take long and he could use Beth's car to go around to the cottage from the road.

Ariana looked up and called after him, "Yeah, no problem. We've had five more sales. Don't know what you're doing but it's working."

He didn't answer. She wandered into the main gallery to speak with him, but the thick oak door creaked shut, and he'd shot from there. Just like the day before.

CHAPTER EIGHT

Courtney was fired. She didn't even argue or want to see the video. The jig was up. When Ariana had called Beth about the takings being down again, Beth had checked the camera footage too, and could see Courtney taking cash out of the till and stashing it into her apron. Beth shook her head as she thought about it. You never could tell with staff. It was a shame because she was a nice girl. Plus, it left her short-staffed on the bar again.

She stood at the pass between the kitchen and the restaurant. What was she going to do now? She couldn't ask Rhys to do double shifts. There were one or two waiting on staff she could use at a push. Lisa was her best junior waitress, but she was a bit young, being only seventeen. She was also really good at the tables, so she didn't want to really put her onto the bar.

"Penny for them?"

"Eh?"

"Penny for your thoughts," Paul said wandering up to her.

"I was just thinking about who we could put on the bar now I've lost Courtney," Beth answered.

Paul stood for a good minute thinking and tapping a pen on the pass, which irritated the Hell out of Beth. She stared at the pen and he stopped.

"Sorry."

They had a great set up by now, with lots of college students training to be chefs, working apprenticeships or as a day release options to gain experience.

"What if we put the bar into the chef training programme?" Paul finally suggested.

"That could work…"

Beth pursed her lips in thought. She wanted to know more.

"Anyone who wants a career in the restaurant trade needs to learn about customers, and what it's like to be out on the floor, right? Otherwise, they start playing up and getting all arsey about customer requests."

Beth snorted. She'd seen that too many times; jumped up chefs sounding off just because someone had asked for something a little off the menu.

"Keep going," she told him.

"So... learning the bar's a great skill for the trainees, and from what I've seen Rhys is about as good a barman as you can get. I can see how he works with the waiting on staff, they really respect him, and he runs a tight ship. What about we get him to train our chefs up? They could rotate onto the bar in the day when it's quieter."

"Hmmm. Sounds good. I'll fly it by him," Beth agreed. This was why she enjoyed working with Paul.

"In the meantime, I can get Dan to help out on the bar instead of waiting on, and get him trained up to fill in."

Dan was Paul's nineteen-year-old son. The eldest of his two boys, Dan had left school last year. He was a hard-working boy, who'd been helping Gareth with building jobs for a couple of years and worked in the restaurant in the evenings, waiting on tables. He was popular with the customers, and all the physical construction work, plus the fitness training he was doing, was helping him to get fit. The plan he'd formulated with Paul was for him to join up for the army in the autumn, and hopefully become a Paratrooper, like his Dad had been.

"Give Dan a call and we'll give him a go on the bar tonight with Rhys," Beth confirmed.

When Beth flew it by him, Rhys thought training the chefs on the bar was an excellent idea too and was looking forward to it. Beth counted herself lucky for Rhys' arrival and his help. Although she understood his reasons why, she was sad to hear that he was moving out of the boathouse. He was right, it would be better for him to have his own space, and the boathouse would be small once the little one made an appearance. Nevertheless, she would miss him. It'd been fun having him around.

Beth smiled to herself, wondering what Ariana thought about the new arrangement. She'd been all too clear what she felt about Rhys, even though they seemed to be getting along better now, she observed. Beth hadn't seen any of the arrogance in Rhys that Ariana had complained about. She watched him showing Dan the ropes. He was great with people. She'd heard all about how he'd handled the steak complaint, he was a charmer, *alright*. *So* different to Gareth, who was stoic and hard to read, but then she *loved that* about her husband.

"Alright, Rhys. How's it going, *man*?"

Adam Williams, one of Rhys' high school friends, was at the bar.

"Not bad, *la*."

Rhys greeted him warmly enough. He hadn't seen him since he was eighteen, but knew only too well what he'd been like back then. He wasn't about to be drawn into the same lifestyle choices now.

"Buzzin'. I'll have three pints of lager and one cider, mate. You back here for good?"

"Not sure yet,' Rhys answered evasively. "What you up to these days?"

"This and that. Mainly *that*; I'm not gonna lie to ya. Doing alright though," Adam replied.

He flashed the Mercedes badge of the car keys he was playing with in his hand, so Rhys knew exactly what he was driving.

Flash git! Adam hadn't changed one bit, Rhys thought, as he guided Dan on how to pour the drinks.

"Tip the glass a bit more to control that froth, Dan."

Rhys was watching him pour his first pint of lager.

"*Tidy*. That's it. Hey, that's a great first pint."

Dan beamed.

Rhys served Adam the drinks and took the money.

"Catch you later, yeah? Come over if you get a break," Adam said.

He pointed his head towards a table outside, where there were a group of three men smoking. Rhys didn't know them, but it was a bit chilly to be sitting outside yet. Most people just went out for a smoke at this time of year, only the very hardy braved the weather all evening.

"It's pretty busy here. If I can, I will."

As Adam walked away with a tray of drinks, he passed Ariana. Rhys could see him speaking to her. She lifted her chin at him in response and gave him a hard stare. Rhys sniggered silently to himself. It was good to know that he wasn't the *only* one Ariana had issues with. He didn't know what Adam had done to wind her up, but she sure looked mean for a good while after he'd gone outside with the drinks.

So, army, eh?" Rhys asked Dan.

"Hopefully. I'm working hard on my fitness and getting some cash to do a bit of travelling before I go in. Dad would only agree if I took a year off after school to make sure I was making the right choice. He did fifteen years, so he knows what I'm in for," Dan explained.

"Once you sign on that dotted line, they own your butt, Danny Boy."

Dan agreed but his attention was wandering. Rhys saw that his eyes were fixed on one of the waiting on girls, who was joking with a customer she was serving. Rhys' face broke into a smirk. Lisa was a pretty girl with a curvy figure and long, straight blonde hair. And judging by Dan's mooning manner, he was heavily into her.

"Earth to Dan," Rhys nudged him.

"Sorry."

Dan was back in the room.

"Hey, don't apologise. Joys of standing behind the bar. You get to survey the land from time to time. Just keep your focus, eh," Rhys reminded him.

"Can I ask you something? Something personal."

Dan stood by his side not looking at Rhys, but Rhys could tell that Dan was straining beyond his comfort zone.

"Oh, okay," Rhys answered dubiously.

"How do you get girls to ask you out all the time?"

Rhys nearly choked.

"I saw Courtney drooling over you. Then there was that girl at the bar last night, the one who wouldn't go home. Even *Ariana's* giving you gifts... How do you do it, man?" Dan asked, grinning at him.

"Aw, Danny boy, *as you know,* I didn't go with Courtney *or* the drunk girl last night."

"Hmm," Dan agreed staring at Lisa across the restaurant floor. "I've been wanting to ask Lisa out for ages."

"I guess you've got to be a bit fearless. Try some flirting," Rhys answered helpfully. "But, the biggest thing Dan, is to be nice to her. Get to be her friend. Then either she'll be into you *or not*."

He looked over at Ariana. Was *she* into him, or not, he wondered?

Through the evening, the more Rhys watched Adam and his crew, the less he liked what he was seeing. Periodically, in pairs, they'd slip to the toilet. Rhys knew that meant only one thing. He could also see the car park from the front window; every now and then, a car would pull up, with a single driver in it. He watched as one of Adam's friends talked to the driver through the front car window before the car pulled away.

"Ariana?" Rhys called her over. "You got any of that lip balm Gwen makes, on you?"

"Need a bit of male grooming do ya, George Clooney?" she barbed. "Protect that Hollywood smile of yours from the vicious Welsh winds."

She went over to the staff changing area and fished out a flat tin of Gwen's geranium beeswax lip balm from her handbag, which she

67

brought back over to Rhys. My God, was he *really* that vain? She watched in disbelief as he took it from her and disappeared into the toilets, emerging five minutes later.

"Check you haven't got any on your teeth, Johnny Depp," she taunted.

He handed her back an almost empty box.

"What the Hell?"

"Sorry. I'll pay for a new one from Gwen... Dan, you okay on the bar for a sec?"

Dan nodded and Rhys disappeared into the kitchen to find Beth and Paul.

When he told her, she couldn't believe what she was hearing. Not here. Not in *her* restaurant.

"You sure about this?" Beth asked.

"Hundred per cent. I've been watching them all night," Rhys replied.

"Beth, you're in no condition to confront them." Paul stepped in to stop her stomping off up to them right there and then; bump and all.

"We should get the police involved."

"We've got no hard evidence though," Beth argued. "Can't we sort this ourselves? Put the frighteners on them."

Taking coke in the toilets and doing drug deals from the car park! This was meant to be a small seaside village, a piece of paradise.

"Keep the toilet tops and sinks greased from now on," Rhys advised.

Paul flexed his muscles. His years in the military meant he wasn't going to put up with these small-town jerks. And he certainly wasn't going to let them affect the reputation of the place they were working so hard to build.

"Rhys, you know one of them. *Adam*, you said? Let's go for a chat."

Rhys nodded and made for the back door of the kitchen, alongside him.

"Take care."

Beth watched them walking around the deck to the outside table, closest to the car park where Adam and his three chums were sat.

Paul and Rhys approached them. Carefully assessing the situation as he walked, Paul saw that two of the four men looked quite young, more his son's age, late teens, early twenties. They were wiry but smaller than he was. Easy to take down, if he had to. The two others were more of a problem. Adam was tall and built, he looked like he worked out. The other guy didn't look very fit, but he was a big lad too, and probably could put some weight behind a punch.

"Enjoying your evening, lads?"

Paul and Rhys neared the table.

"What's it to you?" the big lad to Adam's left threw back at him.

"We were enjoying a quiet drink until you two disturbed our peace," Adam said with a hint of menace in his voice, "Unless you've come to join us, Rhys?"

It was a challenge. Rhys stood shoulder to shoulder with Paul, and neither flinched.

Paul eyeballed Adam steadily.

"We know what the score is. We've been watching you all night. I'm gonna make this real clear. The dealing, snorting coke in the bogs. You're not welcome here. Finish up and leave."

Paul spoke calmly and authoritatively as he towered over them seated at the table.

"This is bollocks," Adam said quietly.

He examined Paul; evaluating the size of him, considering for a long moment what to do next.

Suddenly, without warning, he snatched his half-full pint of lager off the table and flung it violently at the stone paving in front of Paul's feet, splashing Paul's legs and smashing it into a shower of glass fragments. The muscle in Paul's cheek twitched, but both he and Rhys stood firm, fists tightened but arms to their side. They were not going to be provoked into a fight. Adam used the diversion to spring up from the table to his full height, squaring up to Rhys, aggressively.

"Place's a dump anyway. Someone should put a torch to it."

Rhys' biceps tightened as he tensed his arms, ready to swing a punch if Adam started.

Paul stood solid, muscular and firm, not backing away, not starting any moves either. They were still four against two and creating more of a scene outside the restaurant was not on.

He stared Adam down.

"You threatening us?"

Adam hesitated and seemed to think better of the situation. He took in the army tattoos and the protruding biceps of his mahogany, taut arms. He cocked his head and indicated silently to the others that it was time to leave. They took their cue from their leader and slammed their glasses to the ground too. One smashed, two bounced and hit Ariana's foot as she walked from the front restaurant door towards the table.

Adam noticed her arrival and shouted over to her cockily,

"Ariana honey... any time you wanna fuck again, you call me, yeah?"

Ariana froze. Stunned.

If he could have, he would have decked him right there. *The bastard!* Rhys' vision blurred in rage as he began to spin round to jump Adam from behind.

Luckily, Paul's quick reactions anticipated the move and he grabbed Rhys back by the shoulders and held him firm until all four men were safely in Adam's white Mercedes sport's car, and the engine had started up. Adam revved it high, and screeching and spinning the wheels as he pulled away, he drove out of the car park.

"I will kill him if he ever talks about Ariana like that again, so help me God," Rhys vowed angrily to Paul. "Not a word about this, please."

Paul nodded back solemnly.

Ariana was mortified. How could he have done that to her? She rushed back into the restaurant before the car had even left and sped straight to the ladies' toilets where she sat with her head in her hands for ten minutes, cooling down. What would Rhys think of her now, she despaired? Adam had made her sound like a slut.

Satisfied that the car wasn't coming back, Paul and Rhys wandered back into the restaurant, and over to the pass where Beth had taken over the service. It had quietened down, and she was just finishing the last main meal order, directing the junior chefs.

"How'd it go?" she asked, concerned.

Paul and Rhys looked at each other in silent agreement. They were not going to mention the threat Adam had made just yet. He was angry, he was an idiot, a small-town drug dealer.

"No problems, we've banned them."

Paul went over to the back to speak with a kitchen junior who discreetly disappeared out the back door with a brush and pan to clear up the glass before Beth noticed.

Beth watched Rhys as he went back to the bar. He was staring at Ariana. She thought he looked pained. He definitely still had a thing for her, she was sure. And Ariana? Well, Miss Cool was avoiding all eye contact and keeping as far apart as she possibly could from him, Beth observed. She'd never seen Ariana so awkward and on edge. She was usually so composed. He was ruffling her feathers alright.

Bianca: Hey Luc, saw you were online

Luc: Yeah. How you doing?

Rhys was typing in the studio on Ariana's wifi. He could see her bedroom light from the sofa where he was typing. If she found out the truth, he'd be toast.

Bianca: Confused. I really need to talk

Luc: Sure. What's up?

Bianca: I don't know if I can tell you. Oh God!!!

Luc: Why not? You know you can tell me anything

Bianca: It's so complicated

Luc: Try me

Bianca: I'm all over the place

Luc: Spill it, Bianca

Bianca: Well there's this guy

Luc: Your ex?

This should be interesting, Rhys thought.

Bianca: How did you guess?

Luc: Lucky strike

Bianca: I feel so mixed up. My gran's given him our studio to live in, and he's working with me in the gallery, and it must be my hormones 'cos I just can't stop thinking about him

Luc: Really?

This was interesting news.

Bianca: I told you this was a mistake. Talking like this to you. Now you'll hate me too

She was right. This was a mistake. He felt like a total jerk. It was like reading her diary or listening to girl talk.

Luc: I could never hate you, Bianca. I owe you so much

Bianca: It gets worse tho'. His tosser of a mate, Adam, turned up tonight and told the world I shagged him. I just wanted to die, I was so embarrassed

Luc: Did you?

Bianca: Die?

Luc: NO! Shag him?

Bianca: Yeah. One big regret one night. Just after Rhys

Rhys paused. Had that doofus been her first? This online chat was so wrong on so many levels. And who was he to judge Ariana? If she only knew about all his one-night stands. He'd been far worse than her, he knew that.

71

Luc: Ahhh, don't beat yourself up about it

Bianca: We all have a past, right? What about you?

Luc: Yeah, definitely me too

Bianca: Bet my ex thinks I'm a slut now

Luc: Nah. Bet he's kicking himself for being such a douche and losing you first time around

Bianca: How'd 'you know that?

Luc: 'Cos I'm a guy. And that's how I'd be

Bianca: He did try and defend me against Adam, I s'pose

Luc: See. He likes you

Bianca: Y'think?

He needed to close down Luc. He should try to do that now.

Luc. Uh-huh. Bianca, there's no getting around this. I'm in the States and you're in the UK. I'm just out of rehab. I think you should explore these feelings you have for your ex and see how it goes

*Bianca: **You do???***

Rhys thought she sounded disappointed.

Luc: It hurts my heart, but yes. Bianca, you need to have a life

Bianca: But Luc?

Luc: When all's said and done, we're only keyboard buddies. We're so far apart

Bianca: How can you say that!

Luc: Bianca, I'm like a ghost in your life. But, your ex, he's real

There was a long pause while Ariana thought about Luc's words.

Bianca: You sure?

Luc: Yes Bianca. If you need me, I'll always be here for you. Any time

Bianca: Thanks x

She signed off. Rhys thought it sounded curt. She was probably annoyed with Luc now too. He didn't feel like sleeping yet; he'd always been a night owl. He made a cup of fruit tea from the kettle Gwen had thoughtfully brought over earlier and crept quietly out and down to the beach. It a cold, clear night with a large white moon that threw a silvery light across the calm waters in the cove. Whatever anyone said, to *him*, Wales was still the most beautiful place. Sitting out, watching and listening to the lapping ripples of the tranquil sea, it was so restful. At his lowest points, he'd been conflicted about coming home, scared about confronting his failure and lies, he now realised. Sitting here, he felt home had helped him lift him out of the darkness that had been consuming him. It had re-energised him. He was feeling well; his sick mind was healing. He needed this time each day; thinking, relaxing, meditating.

Ariana was irritated. No; she was flat out *pissed off*. Had Luc just dumped her? Did he *mean* it? It was disappointing; she thought she meant more to him than *that*. It was probably because she'd told him about Rhys, she reasoned. Deep down, she knew Luc was right, but it was *bloody* annoying. They *were* only online friends, but she didn't need to hear that right now. Not when she was trying to explain to him about how confused she was, and how upset she'd been about what Adam said, in front of him.

Looking out of her bedroom window at the full moon on the sea, Ariana noticed a shadow on the beach. It was Rhys; there, on the shore, with a mug in his hand. It looked so lovely out there, so peaceful. She needed to clear her mind too, and maybe talk to him about Adam. After much deliberation, she summoned her courage, put on her jacket and walked down to the cove. She hoped Gwen wouldn't hear her creeping around. She'd long gone to bed though, so Ariana thought she was probably safe.

Rhys looked up as he heard a movement behind him. Ariana dropped down to sit beside him on the driftwood log. He stretched his arm loosely around her shoulder. She bristled at first, but she let it rest there. It felt so good. Neither of them spoke for an age.

"What was happening tonight, with Adam and his mates?" Ariana asked, finally breaking the silence between them, hoping she could clear the air about it.

"I saw him dealing in the car park and they were doing coke in the toilets," Rhys answered.

"Ah, you used my lip balm to grease the cistern and sinks."

It made sense now. Rhys squeezed her shoulder.

"Turns out my lips weren't chapped after all, and I'm not that vain, *honest*," he shrugged, smiling.

"Adam's not someone you want to mess with," Ariana warned.

"He knows where he stands now," Rhys said softly.

"You know the thing he said about me?" she broached tentatively.

He turned to her, gazing into her eyes. She shuddered and her heart raced. He took her hand and studied her Claddagh ring, drawing circles over the back of her hand with his thumb.

"Ariana, we've all got a past. *Me,* more than anyone. Let's only look forward, yeah?"

She smiled, relieved, and turned her attention back to the sea, sitting in silence for a while, enjoying the peacefulness of the night with Rhys wrapped around her, still holding her hand.

"Where do you go every day?" Ariana uttered quietly. "In the afternoons?"

Rhys studied the waters in front of them, considering. He didn't reply at first and then, after a little while longer, said finally,

"A.A. I'm in recovery. It's a group meeting."

Rhys drank in her air of surprise. She hadn't expected that, he could tell.

"That's why I need *you* not to judge me and only to look forward too. I've been pretty fucked up recently. But now I'm much better; sober and clean... but I'm still a work in progress, Ari."

Ariana leaned into his shoulder.

"I have a friend who's just out of rehab too."

Was that an invitation to tell her more?

Rhys sniffed.

"I can't talk about it yet. I will. I'll tell you *everything,* I promise. But not tonight."

Ariana didn't push it further. She touched his leg in reassurance.

"I'm trying to get better. But it's not always easy," he said softly.

Ariana stared out at the sea.

"Seeing Adam tonight. You *are* a different person now, Rhys."

His chest filled. That meant a lot.

"Thank you."

She heard the emotion crackle in his voice.

He drew her closer to him as she rested her head on his shoulder. He longed to kiss her but how could he, knowing how he was still tricking her? Was he a better person? She didn't really know him at all. He needed to be honest with her, but she'd freak if she knew everything.

"You'll get there, Rhys."

She edged away from him and then surprised him as she pivoted around, and dropped a fleeting kiss, her lips grazing against his lightly before she stood up and walked back towards the cottage.

"Yeah. I will. One day at a time."

Maybe that platitude *was* all that there was to say.

CHAPTER NINE

"Two months sober. Well done, Rhys."

Owen clasped a strong arm around his brother's shoulder.

"It feels good," Rhys confessed. "Thanks, man, for the other day."

Owen had come up from Cardiff to see him and they were taking a walk around the lower lambing fields before lunch. Madog had been out the night before and was feeling the worse for wear. David had fed the sheep and milked, and Owen, with a reluctant Rhys in tow, had offered to do a check on the maternity wing, the sheep in the lower fields who were about to lamb.

Ellen was busy in the kitchen making everyone a family lunch. Gareth and Beth were coming over and she was making a roast beef dinner with all the trimmings.

"So; what next?"

Owen was curious. Rhys had come back but what were his plans? Owen knew, as a psychologist, how important goals were, but it was still early days for Rhys, and he didn't want to push him too far.

"Not sure. A bit of time out, and then maybe go for some auditions in the autumn? Right now, I'm not sure I can handle rejection too well," Rhys admitted truthfully.

"Yeah, I know what you mean."

Owen was fighting to keep his place in the national team. At thirty, he'd taken a fair few knocks, and was currently out of action for his country and his club for four weeks with a back injury. The physio team told him training was out, but he needed to keep moving. Walk, swim but definitely no weights, and no contact sports. There were talented young guns snapping at his heels from the club sides, ready to take his rugby position in a heartbeat. Being an elite athlete wasn't going to last forever, and that scared him more than he cared to admit. It was all he'd ever wanted to do, and without rugby, there would be a gaping hole in his life.

The sheep were all fine; although there was one ewe who was looking for a quiet place near the fence and pawing the ground with her hoof. It was a sign that she was going to lamb. They were walking back, past the sheds to the house when Rhys' phone went off. It was Gareth. Owen tried to listen in but couldn't pick up the thread of what was being said.

"Take care and drive safe…. Yeah, no problem. Leave it with me."
Rhys ended the call.

"The baby's coming," he explained as he put his phone back in his pocket.

He walked into the farm kitchen with Owen. Ellen greeted her boys with a motherly, proud look. It was so rare to have them all home.

"Gareth's just called. Beth's gone into labour. He's driving her to the hospital now. He wants some help with the restaurant service, it's packed and Beth's stressing. Sorry, Mam; I'm gonna have to take a rain check on lunch."

Ellen was disappointed but she understood. She was used to emergency callouts on the farm.

"Oh okay. No problem."

She hoped that Beth would be alright. She was a tough cookie, and the last time Gareth rushed her to the hospital, it was with an emergency ectopic pregnancy. She prayed that it all would go smoothly this time around.

Madog, who sat at the table looking very hungover, looked away and stared into space. There was no sugar-coating it. Two years on, and he still found talk of childbirth difficult. Little Jake was a blessing, but he'd lost Caitlin on the operating table after having him. She'd only been twenty-four years old.

He coughed and rose up from his seat, "Just need to check the dogs."

David's eyes followed him as he left. His eyes met Ellen's in a brief acknowledgement of the pain and sadness that boy still felt every day.

Rhys got ready to leave.

"What's this I hear about you living in Gwen Jones' garden shed?"
Ellen chose her moment to strike.

"The view's better from there, than the farm, Mam." Owen teased.

Rhys shot Owen a dirty look. Brothers were meant to have each others' backs.

"Mmm. It wouldn't have anything to do with a certain Freshwater Bay artist would it?"

Even David had started now.

Everyone laughed and Rhys grinned.

"No comment."

"Ari, can you help me?"

Ariana was sitting on a rock at the top of the beach sketching the shape of the wave as it broke when Rhys came jogging up from the path over to her.

"Yeah sure."

She looked a little flustered when she saw him.

"Beth's gone into labour and we need to give them a hand in the restaurant this afternoon. There's over a hundred booked in, and Beth's worried Paul and the others won't cope."

Ariana nodded. She'd do whatever they wanted. They made their way back to the cottage and got changed quickly into their work uniforms. Ariana made chicken and salad sandwiches for them, and they both ate it hurriedly in the kitchen. It was going to be a long shift.

"We look like sailors," she laughed, looking at him in his striped t-shirt sitting opposite her at the kitchen table.

"I gotta talk to Beth about this uniform. What's wrong with a black T-shirt?"

"I dunno, I've worn worse."

Ariana laughed, "Occupational hazard?"

"Yeah. Try turning up for work every day in a codpiece," Rhys joked.

"*Ahh*, don't you just love Shakespeare."

They walked along the path up to the restaurant. It was blustery and fresh, and the waves licked up in tongues out of the ocean below making the perfect curls that Ariana had been trying to sketch before Rhys turned up. The shape inspired a new design that was bubbling away in her brain. Rhys took her hand as they passed alongside the sheer drops. She didn't let go and he kept on to it, way past the most dangerous sections right until they reached Freshwater Bay village. Was she indeed between the devil and the deep blue sea, she wondered to herself?

The contractions that had started sporadically early that morning, were now coming thick and fast, each time filling Beth with crippling pain. Gareth's face was full of panic when he realised that this was *it*. They needed to get to the hospital. Both of them were haunted by their last visit there when Beth had to have emergency surgery.

"I'm scared, Gareth," Beth whispered quietly to him as she got into the pickup. "What if something's wrong, like the last time?"

He leant over from his seat, and kissed her tenderly, "It'll be alright *cariad*. Everything will be okay. I'll be with you the whole time and I'm *never* letting you go."

He squeezed her hand and got the truck moving, driving quickly to the hospital, which was around an hour's drive away.

As they stepped into La Galloise both Ariana and Rhys knew straight away that things were out of control. Paul was barking orders in the kitchen, trying to keep things together as the row of order checks were stacking up on the pass. There were too many tables with dirty plates still on them, and a number of customers who were starting to look around, a sign that they'd been waiting too long for their food.

"We're here to help."

Paul looked at them as if a prayer had been answered.

"No more orders please, we're catching our tails back here."

He pushed four plates hurriedly to Dan, who was waiting on. Lisa was also around but was struggling to pacify a couple of tables who were starting to ask about the wait for food.

"How d'you want to play this?" Rhys asked Ariana.

"You're great with the customers. How 'bout you manage the seating and any complaints, keep everyone happy, and I'll get the tables straight and manage the waiting on staff?"

They set into action. Rhys triaged the tables, and Ariana got Lisa and Dan making any drinks and desserts that needed to be done. She set on to clearing some tables and getting food out from the kitchen. Finding a bag of part-cooked frozen bread rolls, she slammed a tray of them into one of the ovens.

Meanwhile, Rhys was working the tables and talking to customers casually, helping to relax the vibe, making the place less febrile as the waiting on staff rushed around purposefully. He gave one table, who had waited forty-five minutes, a round of free drinks, and worked with Paul to get their food out quickly. He managed to hold speculative customers and booked in customers at the bar, and within half an hour, things were manically busy, but the restaurant was under control. Ariana put together complimentary baskets of bread rolls with oils and dips for any table with a wait, and with Dan and Lisa backing her up, the place was soon straight, and they were back on track. The breathing space and help were appreciated by Paul, who was working like a machine and trying to keep his trainees calm and focussed, check by check.

"Was I glad to see you two."

Paul wiped his brow.

"Thought we were going under back there."

"You were. Rhys, he sorted it," Ariana said gratefully.

"Seems to me like you both made a great team."

Paul winked at Rhys, and Ariana coloured up.

As the evening shift drew to a close, the whole crew felt they had been in a war. They were a band of brothers who had pulled together and had gotten through; battle-weary but unscathed.

Rhys watched Dan and Lisa and the smouldering looks they gave each other as they worked. When Ariana gave them both a short break, he saw them talking to each other out on the deck, and they were both laughing. Things seemed to be going pretty well for Danny Boy, he thought to himself, pleased. He was a good kid. Dan sauntered up to the bar a little later, a huge grin plastered on his face.

"Rhys. Thanks, man."

"Huh?"

Rhys was unloading a tray of glasses.

"Lisa," he beamed. "I'm taking her out this week."

"Buzzin'."

"Can I ask you something else?" Dan asked a little unsure.

"Hey, if you want us to have the *talk*. Forget it. Speak to your dad," Rhys chuckled.

Dan grabbed a cloth and flicked it at Rhys' face, who saw it coming and dodged it just in time.

"Jesus, Rhys! I'm nearly nineteen, not twelve."

"Twelve? Things start *that* early, these days?"

"No. I wanted to ask if you'd give us a hand with our sketch for the Young Farmers' competition."

Rhys knew that these were fiercely fought. Rival groups from rural communities wrote and then performed their own drama sketches, competing against each other to win the prize. The sketches were usually hilarious, topical and as brutal as you'd expect from a group of teenagers. There were huge dollops of pride involved. He'd been in them too when he was a kid and they'd been an important part in helping him to learn his craft. It was a tradition that he was passionate to keep going here when so many other rural community traditions were disappearing fast.

"Is it for the regionals?" Rhys asked.

"Yeah. I can email you the script. It's pretty shaky. We *truly* suck. I think we need a director," Dan answered honestly.

"I can come and take a look?" Rhys offered.

"*Awesome!* Tuesday night at seven in the village hall. They're gonna be so *stoked* when they hear we've got a Hollywood actor directing us," Dan said excitedly.

"Hey, Dan? Leave out the Hollywood bullshit, yeah?" Rhys cut in.

"Oh, okay."

Dan put the drinks Rhys had just filled onto a tray.

"I don't mind helping, but I don't want everyone blagging my head."

"Sure, man. Whatever. Thanks again, yeah."

Dan took the tray out to the table.

"No worries."

Things were quiet; last orders had been called a while back, and one last table of drinkers were finishing off their drinks when Gareth walked into La Galloise, looking like he'd been through the fire too. Rhys at the bar, saw him as he came in, and went over to him anxiously.

"We've got us a boy. He's so perfect," he said, his voice thick.

Seeing his brother, Gareth was overcome with emotion. He'd held it together all day with Beth. She'd been amazing; so powerful and strong as she dug deep and helped his little man enter the world.

"Ahh, Gareth!" Rhys drew him into a tight bear hug and slapped his back.

"Hey, Ari!" Rhys called her over. "Beth's had a boy!"

Ariana cheered and rushed in too with kisses and hugs.

Paul heard and came over too, giving Gareth's hand a vigorous shake.

Rhys went back behind the bar and poured Gareth a generous finger of malt whisky.

Gareth received it gratefully.

"It was unbelievable," he told them, "Best day of my life. He's so perfect. We're calling him Finn. I can't get over it. I'm a father."

"Finn, huh? I like that," Rhys considered.

He had never really thought that much about children before. But seeing Gareth there, so proud, so complete, he started to wonder. Would *he* ever become a dad? These things happened to people with normal lives, not to flaky actors. He looked at Ariana. Maybe it was time to try to find something more solid? Going off, touring theatres with a play may not be the best plan for him.

"How's Beth? Eight pounds ten ounces, you say? *Oww.* That musta hurt." Ariana screwed up her nose.

"Yeah, it took some doing, let me tell ya. It was too late for an epidural. She's resting now and the nurses sent me home for the night. She's hoping to be out of there by tomorrow afternoon."

Gareth's shoulders relaxed as the amber liquid burned his throat.

"One down fourteen more to go," Rhys laughed as he reminded him about his rugby team.

"Hmm, think Beth may have something to say about that. Judging by what she was screaming in labour. She's probably booking me in for the snip right now."

"Cup of tea?" Ariana asked Rhys as they walked back to the cottage after closing up. It was late, just after midnight but she knew they were both buzzing after the busy shift.

"Sounds good. Fancy a bit of fresh air?"

They made a mug of tea each and carried it down to the driftwood log on the beach. It was so quiet, the wind had dropped and though it was still chilly, it was pleasant to sit. The tide was in and it came right up the beach.

He put his arm around Ariana, and they sat in silence watching and listening to the waves gently lapping the shore. Rhys' heart was full. In that moment, sitting there with Ariana. He'd knew now that he was home.

She propped her head against his broad chest and reclined into him. He felt so good, and her heart beat faster. Putting down his mug, he gently stroked her hair and she closed her eyes, feeling the tranquillity of the moment.

"I can't believe Beth and Gareth are now parents. When she first came here, they hated each other. He accused her of being a gold digger when she first inherited the restaurant."

"Do you still hate me, Ariana?" Rhys asked her softly.

A smile floated across her face.

"Have you seen my bank balance? Thanks to you my sales are going through the ceiling. I'm working flat out now on getting stock for the summer."

"But am I forgiven? I'm not that kid anymore," Rhys pressed.

Ariana noted the touch of concern in his voice. He really did care what she thought. She pivoted around to face him, God he was so handsome, she thought, as she studied him closely in the shadowy light.

"I can see that. Yes, you're forgiven," she smiled at him, looking into his eyes briefly before she looked away shyly.

"I've actually got a surprise for you."

She produced a pair of tickets from her coat pocket.

"I checked; we're not working."

Rhys took a ticket and tried in vain to make out the words in the darkness.

"It's Taming of the Shrew, a live broadcast of the Royal Shakespeare Company production in the theatre in Swansea," she said, seeing that he was struggling to read it.

Taming of the Shrew? Rhys' lips curled as he contemplated the irony of that. He held her hand and gazed into her eyes.

"It's midweek, so we can both go. I checked with Paul. I'll drive," she said, brushing her hair away from her face, tilting her chin up towards him slightly, a little defiantly, protecting herself in case he rejected her gift again.

"Thank you, Ariana. That's really sweet of you. Yes, I'd love to go."

He lightly touched her face and stroked her cheek before leaning over and brushing her lips gently with his; unsure of how she would react. He felt her gasp as he delicately and sensuously kissed her. His hand circled her waist and he pulled her into him, closer. She responded to him tentatively at first, and then with more certainty, deepening the kiss, feeling him first with the tip of her tongue, and then with velvet strokes as their tongues tangled together. She thrummed with the simmering passion that was rippling through her, a prelude to the flames of desire she knew she still had for him, locked away.

She tasted so delicious, he could feel the deep cravings within her, below the veneer of shyness she had about her. It was sexy as Hell. He was on fire; his body was so hard for her, he was consumed. He longed to move his mouth along her neck, feel those full breasts pressing against him. *But dammit!* He couldn't go further yet. He needed to take

82

it slow. She'd run a mile if he told her the truth, that he wanted to jump her bones, right here on the beach. Ariana was special. He'd disrespected her once before; *no way* was he doing that again. An involuntary sigh parted from her as he ended the most passionate kiss of his life. He was a goner. He wanted her and not just for now. He wanted her mouth on him, always.

"*Uhh*, I think I'd better get going. I've got to make the first post tomorrow."

She moved out of the embrace as he leaned back away from her, her fingers still entwined in his. He noted her shaky breath and the note of embarrassment as she spoke. He loved the slight awkwardness about her when she was out of her comfort zone.

"I'm going to sit here for a bit. I'll see you tomorrow. Sweet dreams, Ariana."

She let go of his hand and cocked her head. Was it her imagination, or did he sound just like Luc?

CHAPTER TEN

Rhys' life was suddenly busy, he realised. The days were spent helping Ariana run the gallery, and this week alone he was training staff up on the bar, helping the drama group and there was the trip to the theatre with Ariana, which he was looking forward to. So, when Gareth mentioned going back to the rugby club, he wasn't sure if he could fit it in. Plus, he was worried about the drinking culture. He side-stepped the offer. He needed to keep away from temptation, and the last thing he needed was to wrangle with the boys over why he wasn't knocking back the shots and pints of lager with them.

Rhys and Ariana had closed the gallery early and were over at the boathouse. Neither mentioned the night before, but their fingers interlaced together as they walked the path to the gallery, and they chatted like nothing had happened at the beach. He wasn't sure if that meant that it wasn't going to happen again, or if she was playing it cool. Who could tell with Ariana? Whatever it was, he was going to take this one real slow. She was far too special to him to lose again.

Gareth had just gotten Beth home after her hospital stay and she was rocking Finn to sleep after his feed. Beth handed him over to Gareth, who took him like a pro, Rhys thought. Gareth had got him winded and sleeping in no time, and with no sick down his back. The guy was a natural. Gareth handed the sleeping bundle to Rhys on the sofa, although Rhys could see that he was still hovering. He wasn't going to let Finn out of his sight. He took the baby tentatively, praying that he wouldn't wake up and incur the wrath of his big brother.

Rhys bent over and whispered down to the little sleeping face peeking out from the swaddling blanket, "Croeso i'r teulu, Finn bach." *Welcome to the family, little Finn*. He gently rocked him as Finn slept on, contented with a full belly of milk.

"You okay?" Ariana asked Beth.

"Can I do anything for you? Get you anything?"

"No, it's fine. Gareth got supplies before he picked me up. I have industrial quantities of nappies."

Ariana's eyes drifted over to the brothers as she talked to Beth. She tried to suppress her screaming hormones when she saw how hot Rhys looked with little Finn in his arms by going over to the kitchen island and sticking the kettle on. What had happened to Rhys the rebel, she thought? Ariana started to make them all a cup of tea and she soon had four mugs of what Gwen called 'builder's brew' for everyone; a good strong tea with a splash of milk.

Beth watched amused as Ariana nearly scalded herself, she was so distracted as she made the tea. There was definitely something going on between those two, she was certain of it.

"How did yesterday's service go?"

It was less than twenty-four hours after she'd given birth and Beth's head was back on the business.

"Hmmm… fine," Ariana answered.

"Little bit lively when we first got there. The place was heaving. No dramas though. You need to relax and enjoy your first few days with Finn."

"You tell her, Ariana," Gareth chipped in from the sofa.

Rhys carefully handed Finn back to his dad, who took him eagerly back into his arms.

"Hmm. I think I'm going to need more staff," Beth mused. "Time to call in some favours. I'll see how Alys is fixed."

Things were heating up in the restaurant and she needed another professional she could trust. Alys had worked with her in London but she was now in Paris with one of the best bakers in the business. She had promised Beth two to three weeks, if she could get the holiday time. Beth hated to ask, as Alys needed a break too, but the restaurant was flying. Anyway, she needed to talk to her about some business ideas. It would kill two birds, so to speak.

Rhys caught Ariana's eye and they moved to leave just as Ellen and David were coming in through the door, laden with cake and presents. Ellen rushed in when she saw Gareth with the bundle, and Rhys took his cue to cut and run. He took Ariana's hand and they made a quick exit before Ellen's attention was diverted back to them.

He'd read the script and he was now watching a very ropey sketch performed by a bunch of teenagers, including Dan, as they rehearsed for the Young Farmers drama competition.

What could he say? Rhys didn't want to break their hearts and there were one or two really talented individuals, but where could he start with this? The sketch had taken a popular television reality show, Love Island, where a group of young contestants live in a Spanish island villa and need to couple with different contestants who they can choose to keep, swap or dump. The humour stemmed from them setting the sketch not on the paradise island, but on a Welsh muddy farm, and they had some funny characters in there, each with hilarious quirks and back stories that the audience would relate to and find amusing. It was played for laughs, and the final couple, of course, were the most unlikely match. The old dairy farmer ended up with a glamour model. Rhys thought about it before the rehearsal. It was all a bit flat at the end and very stereotypical.

He gathered them all together.

"Thanks folks. Let's try a few things."

He worked with them a while on developing their characters. Mannerisms and non-verbal cues. Then he paired them up, and they practised reacting to each other's lines. Rhys watched each pair; they were making great progress and it was already much better. They were starting to give each other suggestions, and Rhys guided them further, be more subtle *here*, you need to play that up more *there*.

He drew them back together and got them, even though they were all buzzing and noisy, to simmer down.

"Okay. Can we discuss the ending now?"

Rhys waited for anyone to object, particularly the writer who he saw was sitting with her arms folded and didn't seem too comfortable with any edits at this stage.

"What do you guys honestly think of it now, after what we've been doing tonight?"

"It's alright, I guess."

They started to discuss it.

"Nah man - it sucks. Old farmer, pornstar model. It's kind of a cliché," Dan piped up.

"How could you twist it up? The dairy farmer and the glamour model?" Rhys probed them gently.

"What if she was a vegan?" Mai suggested.

"I like it. What do you think?" Rhys asked the others.

"Yeah and made him grow like chickpeas or quinoa or some veggie shit like that? Grow almond milk and get rid of the cows?" Aled, the main star of the show chirped up.

"That's sick."

The group got going on more suggestions.

"Maybe, she's like, the secret millionaire, and really's some CEO boss woman or something."

"And then, she could like, give him loads of cash to grow almond trees and get rid of the cows."

"Yeah, and get a makeover so he turns into some hot dude."

They worked on it together and soon had a much stronger ending transforming the old farmer into a sexy almond milk grower and the glamour model into a successful angel investor. He was pleased, and so were the group.

"Rhys, man. Can you come to the next rehearsals and the competition?" Aled asked in front of the group.

Rhys rubbed his hand through his hair. He'd really enjoyed working with this lot.

"I'll need to get the dates and check my shifts, but yeah, I'd love to."

His face broke out and filled into a large smile.

"Tidy."

The group, and even the writer, were stoked.

It was so good seeing Alys again. When Alys explained to her Paris boss, another driven female chef, Alys was given unpaid leave to help her friend, and for that Beth would be eternally grateful. Beth insisted she paid her in full and that she take one of the letting rooms above the restaurant. It was still early in the season, and they weren't full by any stretch of the imagination. Alys would do anything required of her, run the restaurant floor, head chef on Paul's nights off; it would allow Beth to have a real switch-off break and give her time to concentrate on Finn.

Alys wandered around the restaurant with Beth, holding little Finn in her arms. She'd been here before, when it first opened, but hadn't seen her friend in over a year. Her life had changed so much compared to when they cheffed together at the London restaurant, La Vie en Rose. Beth had always been ambitious and was a rising star in the culinary world, while Alys had been content to keep learning and focussing on her true passion, the patisserie and bread section. When the opportunity arose to get some experience in one of the world's best bakeries, Alys took it and did the bravest thing of her life. She moved to Paris. The bakery got her a room in an apartment in Montparnasse with another chef. It was tiny but central and close to work. Her French was still a little rudimentary, but she loved living there.

"Talk food to me, Alys," Beth said as they sat by the restaurant window, looking out at the open sea. "What kind of things are you making these days?"

"You'd love this one. How about a Vert Absinthe tart?"

"Eh?"

"It's got a shortbread base with a lemon and mint cream layer, topped with cooked angelica and a green tomato jelly. It's *so* unusual, but absolutely delicious."

Alys was amused as she watched Beth's face as she tried to visualise it and imagine the flavour combos.

"I'll make it for you," she said as she saw Beth struggling to imagine it.

"And they make this beautiful dessert, it's a tart with a biscuit base and a grapefruit cream with, check this out, with rosewater. It's *to die for,* Beth. I've learned so much. And, the owner, she's got two shops and an online business. She's one tough cookie but a real inspiration," Alys gushed.

Beth was in heaven. It was so good, talking food with a fellow geek. Gareth and Freshwater Bay filled her life and she'd never been happier, but every now and again she did miss London. Not the place, just talking with her fellow chefs and tasting inspirational food.

Alys was more than happy to do some training while she was at the restaurant too, and to refresh the dessert menu with Paul. She decided to let her settle in before she mentioned the other reason she'd called Alys. That would keep for now, Beth thought. She'd see how Alys got on. But she still harboured her plan to try and tempt her friend away from Paris and get her here, living and working with her in Freshwater Bay.

Rhys had been looking forward to the trip down to Swansea. He'd spent more days working with Ariana, but what with helping out with the drama and his shifts at the restaurant which hadn't synced with hers, there had been no repeat of the night on the beach, and he was starting to worry that things had cooled off between them. So spending the afternoon in Swansea, getting some food, then an evening in the theatre, was perfect.

They drove Gwen's old SUV down to Swansea. He hoped the old car would make it. It had certainly seen better days and Gwen didn't look like the type of person who regularly serviced it. He checked the oil and the tyres as he filled up with diesel. The back-bumper sticker read

'Adventure before Dementia.' He groaned as he saw people reading it and looking at him puzzled. He was *seriously* going to need to get his shit together and start thinking about buying a car, maybe even a house. That would mean getting something a bit more substantial than bar work and helping out in the gallery for gratis.

In Swansea, Rhys took Ariana to see the Dylan Thomas exhibition, and Ariana took him to Mumbles pier, an old Victorian structure she loved and wanted to photograph. They walked along the bay and ate tapas in a restaurant converted from an old warehouse. The room they ate in had been converted into an old library, wall to wall leather and cloth bound books, lots of candles and a very arty vibe. It was very Ariana. But very Rhys too.

Taming of the Shrew was a live filmed broadcast from Stratford playing to the Swansea theatre. Rhys was intrigued by the format. But it worked. It was immediate and engaging, theatre in film. Ariana was spellbound. She'd never really seen a Shakespeare play before. It had always seemed a bit elite to her, inaccessible. But this play, though set in a vague historical context with traditional costumes, this still felt inclusive, with a diverse cast and modern themes. And there was a character called Bianca. She did a lot of head tossing and was a bit vain and she was being chased by some rich lazy bloke who sent his servant chasing after her... Lucentio.

SHIT! Her head fizzed. Rhys was holding her hand as they were watching it. *The rat!* It was like a bomb going off in her brain. *Rhys was Luc.*

Of course he was. It all made sense now. The failed actor. His ability with her web design and sales. Same interests as Luc, same way of speaking about things. *Oh God!* Same addictions. Her heart pounded. Rhys had been through all that. *Poor baby!* She inadvertently squeezed his hand and he squeezed it back, thinking she was enjoying the play, not thinking about the night he nearly jumped off the bridge.

Jesus! How alone he must have been. Her eyes misted up; she was struggling to concentrate on the play by now. All she wanted to do was taking him home, wrap her arms around him, and hold him, as she had *so* wanted to when he told her where he'd been.

He felt her breathing heavily and put his arm around her, thinking she was engulfed in the emotion of the play.

Did he have the ring too, she wondered? It dawned on her; he knew how she felt about Rhys too. He'd been chatting with her online all the time. *Holy Hell!* That was embarrassing. Her mood swung again, and she bristled. He must have been laughing at her when she was blissfully typing out her innermost secrets to Luc, thinking he was miles away in California. *The bugger.* When he was twenty feet away in the garden shed! But it did, at least, explain why Luc kept defending Rhys, and why Luc had tried to end it when Rhys had come back to Freshwater Bay. *Argh*! she was still thinking of them as two separate people. They were one and the same.

When she'd calmed down a little, she began to process this a bit more. Actually, this was a good thing. She was in love with Luc, they were great friends. She fancied the pants off Rhys. He was Luc. Now she'd got the whole caboodle. But she was still pissed that he'd played her. She thought he'd changed. Maybe he had, but he was still an actor. He still liked to play games. Rhys Morgan, she thought, *I love you, but you are still a rotter!*

As she watched the play, the idea began to take shape. She wanted Rhys and no matter how cheesed off she was with his creation of Luc, she loved him, she knew that. And she'd been through so much with him, she saw how destroyed he'd been by his life in America by his failed career and his addictions. She'd been through the fire with him.

She was so proud that he'd come back and faced up to everyone, that he was turning his life around and that he was still sober and clean. She wanted to be able to talk with him about all of these things, honestly, to help him, and to be with him now in real life. No. She wasn't going to lose him. But she *was* going to make him pay a little for playing her.

Ariana's car pulled in from their car journey back from the theatre. It was late by now and Gwen was in bed, so they made their way quietly back to the cottage. On the path between the kitchen door and the studio, Ariana turned to Rhys to say goodnight.

Tucking a lock of her hair back behind her ear, he covered her mouth with a long, slow, seductive kiss. She responded eagerly and he kissed her ardently, more fervently, exploring her mouth, showing her with his tongue how he wanted to explore the whole of her. They felt so good together, he thought, a perfect fit. Caging around her and sweeping her hair back off her shoulder with his free hand, he feathered hot, insistent, intoxicating kisses down her slender neck, teasing her ear lobe and down onto her collar bone, towards the buttons of her silk blouse.

She pulled away reluctantly.

"Ariana, don't go, stay with me tonight," he whispered into her neck. His hot breath on her ear turned her wild with desire, but she had to keep this together.

She shivered; her brain desperately trying to fight the carnal desires in her body that screamed for her jump him right now. But she had to make him pay, she told herself; she had a plan and she needed to stick to it.

"Rhys, I can't," she breathed, gazing up at his eyes half-lidded with lust.

"Why? Because of Gwen?"

She moved apart but there was no mistaking the hunger in his eyes.

Rhys' arm pulled her back to him, his fingers slipped under her blouse, and she felt them diligently exploring her skin, working their way deliciously around her waist, upwards. His hand was now on her breast and she let out a jagged breath as she felt them slip further under her bra to touch her nipple. She ached with desire. God, how she wanted those hands on her. On *all* of her. Battling with her raw lustful urges as he pressed her closer to him, it took all her might to stop herself from angling towards the hardness she felt against her hips and moving herself up onto him. Her thighs tingled with the anticipation of what her body *so* wanted to have. She knew she couldn't hold out much longer. Another second and she'd be in his bed.

She stepped back from him, exhaling deeply, summoning every ounce of determination she had, as she desperately dammed up the flood of desire that threatened to drown her.

"No."

"Why not?" Rhys' rasped, running his hand through his hair to cool himself off and stop the impulse he had of lifting up, her right now, over his shoulder like a caveman and hauling her off with him into the shed.

"Because I'm in love with someone else."

Rhys was stunned into silence.

"Who?" he managed at last. His voice, low and gravelly.

"You don't know him; he lives in America. His name's Luc."

With all her resolve, she stepped back.

Rhys stared at her. He couldn't believe it. Was he being dumped for *himself*? This was *seriously* fucked up. He had to tell her. *Now.*

"Ariana, we need to talk about this…"

She kissed him lightly on the cheek and quickly bolted towards the cottage door, her back to him, beaming smugly to herself at his shocked reaction.

"I'm so sorry, Rhys. I hope you understand," she called over her shoulder, shutting the door tightly behind her.

Round one goes to Miss Ariana Jones.

What had just happened? What was she doing to him? Rhys made himself a mug of tea. It was seriously late, but his brain couldn't settle. He was feeling the pull for a drink more than ever and was grateful for the late hour or he'd be tempted to go to the Lobster Pot and get smashed. Do a line. No.

Think, he told himself. Keep focussed on this. What should he do? He thought he'd killed Luc off. They hadn't been online since she'd asked advice about him. What if he brought him back and then tried to finish it again? Be more blunt with her this time. Would that work? Would she come back to him then?

He snapped open his laptop. He could see that her bedroom light was still on, too. He wondered if she was online.

Luc: Bianca?

Bianca: Luc, you OK?

Predictable. She knew he was going to chat to her tonight. Rhys' face when she told him she loved Luc. It was a picture, she giggled to herself as she realised how much she was winding him up. He must have a serious case of blue balls.

Luc: Bianca. I think we should end this online chat. It's not healthy for me. You're so far away. I've been talking to my counsellor. I need to move on, live life in the real world. You do too

He *was* dumping her, *the rat!* This was hilarious. How was she going to play this? Outraged and upset? Or cool and detached? What if she manipulated it to try and get him to meet her? Ariana screwed her nose as she thought tactics; finally typing.

Bianca: I love you, Luc. That's real. I'm buying a plane ticket now. I'm coming over to be with you

How would he take that, she wondered?

Luc: No! Don't do that

She squealed as she sensed his panic.

92

Bianca: Why? You married or something? Have you been lying to me all this time?

Luc: God, no!

Bianca: It's OK, then. I can afford the ticket. Let me come to you

Luc: No

Bianca: Tell me why?

Was he going to lie to her? What would his next move be? There was a pause. Ariana watched the screen for a good five minutes as she waited for Luc to reply. In the studio, Rhys was panicking. What if she did fly out? He had to stop her. What was he going to do? Even if he tried to end it, she was sure to try and see him. Should he go up there now and speak with her? No, she'd go ballistic. He could only do one thing. Arrange to meet her face to face and tell her the truth.

Dots finally appeared on the thread; he was typing. She eagerly awaited his next move. Would he finally tell her the truth?

Luc: I'll come to you

Chicken-shit, she told the screen. You should have met me now. But she couldn't help but feel how much she was enjoying this. Playing games was exciting.

Bianca: ?

Silence again. A little lie wouldn't harm, Rhys reasoned to himself. If he told her the truth now, it'd be game over.

Luc: I'll fly over to London

Bianca: You sure?

Luc: Absolutely

Bianca: Want me to come to London?

Luc: Where's best for you?

She could really do without a trip to London. It would take hours by train and cost heaps. She could suggest Freshwater Bay, but that'd be weird, she thought, too close.

Bianca: Cardiff?

Luc: OK. I'll book my flight and be in touch

Had this gone too far now? Should she just call it? Tell him now that the game was up. She could be there now with him, in his arms in the studio. It was so tempting. She remembered how he'd just kissed her, how his lips had explored her neck, his mouth on her ear filling her with tingling sparks of anticipation. No. She needed to teach him a lesson before she could commit to him. If he was going to be hers, there would be no more game playing at her expense. Besides, this was so much fun. She wasn't done with him yet, not by a long chalk.

Bianca: I can't wait to see you, Luc. I'll be dreaming about all the things I want to do to you

Luc: Like? :)

Bianca: Such things! I'll leave you to dream of them too, my love. Goodnight x

Rhys lay back on the bed, covered his face with a pillow and groaned loudly into it. As if he wasn't horny enough before, Ariana Jones was killing him now.

CHAPTER ELEVEN

Ariana buried herself in her work. She plugged herself into her tunes and shut the door. Rhys was running all the sales and the front of house at the gallery by now, and she had to admit it, he was doing a fabulous job. She needed his expertise and help but couldn't handle his company since she'd told him about Luc. She was scared that she'd give her position away, that she'd fall into his arms and *that* would be *that*. And the truth was, she was drawn to him like a magnet. No one had ever made her feel that way. But her heart was still warning her that she needed to be on her guard with him.

Rhys was in a bind. The morning after, he'd tried to talk with her, but she'd gone early to the gallery and was holed up in the workshop for most of the day. His evenings were full of work or drama practices, and even though Ariana lived literally steps away, he seemed to see Gwen more than her, over the next few days.

Finally, he'd succumbed to his lie. He'd been in touch with Ariana online again, and as Luc, he told her that he had booked his plane ticket for next week. They'd agreed to meet in Cardiff in a week's time. How was that going to work? He didn't know yet, but Owen was coming over to meet Finn tomorrow. He was far more sensible than Rhys, he was sure to know what to do, he reasoned.

Ariana came through from her workshop to show him a new piece that she'd just finished. She was wearing a beautiful necklace with an intricate front plate that sat above the collarbone.

"What d'you think?" she said as she modelled it for him, tilting her neck so he could see the design.

"Is that an interlocking knot?" Rhys asked.

She cleared her throat.

"Yeah, a love knot," she said colouring up. "The middle section is my own design, inspired by the waves the other week."

It was intricate and dramatic, curls and sweeps of silver, just like the sea she'd sketched. Rhys was in awe, although he was struggling studying that necklace without being able to put his mouth on her neck.

"Ahh, Ariana that's your best piece yet," he said raspily, trying to keep focussed.

"I've been thinking," he started, trying to make a clean breast of it and telling her the truth.

Ariana looked at him as she tried to unclasp the necklace, it was working, she'd unsettled him. She'd decided to stop avoiding him and give him the opportunity to come clean about Luc. Did she really have to hoick herself all the way to Cardiff so he could man up and admit his lies to her?

"Can you give me a hand with this, please?"

She inadvertently cut him off, turning her back to him. She lifted her hair with both hands, bending her head forward so he could see the necklace clasp and unhook it for her. Rhys cleared his throat. Man, what was she doing to him!

"Uhh... yeah... sure," he tried to sound calm.

Her heart raced as she felt his hands on the back of her neck. The necklace loosened and Rhys remained silent, catching the necklace in his hand as it fell from her.

He changed tack.

"Ariana, I've been thinking. Your web sales are flying, they're super-popular overseas, you can't keep up with sales and soon you'll be out of stock."

"Hmm, I know, I've been trying to come in early, to put in some more hours, but each piece takes so long to make, and I don't want to compromise my designs," she agreed.

"Exactly. So, what d'you think of broadening the range? Buying in some more standard pieces wholesale, then running yours as an exclusive line? You could up the prices on the new designs and create your own exclusive brand; Ariana Jones jewellery, or something."

Rhys looked at her while she considered this. She'd never have thought of that, it was a cracking idea. It'd probably mean a trip to Ireland, maybe even London. The boy had a nose for business, alright.

"Rhys, do you realise how talented you are?"

When Ariana looked into his eyes, he saw her belief in him. He swallowed a hard lump in his throat.

"I wish you'd told them that in Hollywood, I could have done with a cheerleader."

He tried to joke it off.

"Not acting, dumbass. This. You're a genius."

He looked at her confused.

"You've turned around my business and now solved my growing pains without me even telling you. You don't seem to realise it, but you're a helluva businessman. We need to talk about this, and I need to pay you for all the hours you're doing here."

"Ari!" Rhys protested.

"I mean it. How about as my business partner?"

He was a keeper, she thought. She was keeping her distance personally until Cardiff, but she needed him, and this way she got to keep him close.

"Wow. I wasn't expecting that."

Rhys' face broke into a dazzling smile.

"Think about it."

Ariana took the necklace from his hand, her eyes smiling at him flirtatiously.

"Yes, okay, I will."

He wanted her so badly. His stomach churned as he thought nervously about Cardiff, acknowledging to himself the gut-wrenching truth, that losing her would split him in two.

"This place just gets better," Owen said as he watched a hot redhead manage the waiting on staff by the front door.

All four brothers were seated at a table by the window, looking out at the sea. Owen had been meeting Finn for the first time and they met up with Rhys and Madog for lunch at La Galloise. Gareth noticed that Owen's eyes hadn't left Alys for more than a few seconds to glance at the menu.

"I can see Beth's friends are proving a big hit with someone here," Madog teased.

"Forget it, pal, she's only visiting. Anyway, thought you and Julia were still on?" Gareth probed.

Among others, Owen had been dating a sports journalist on and off for just over a year. She was a regular on television spots and they'd met after one of the rugby international games.

"Uhh… things are a little… complex," Owen said evasively.

"She's relocating to London. She's been offered a national TV slot. We have an arrangement. We see other people."

Madog and Rhys looked at each other but didn't question their brother further. It was up to him, but she sounded like she was a high-class booty call or maybe that's what he was?

Gareth took a drink of his lager.

"If it's not right, best to end it. Don't do what I did and drift along," he advised his brother, thinking back to his disastrous first marriage.

"Mmm," Owen agreed distractedly as his eyes examined the diaphanous curves of the redhead.

"So who's the friend?"

"Alys," Rhys confirmed.

Owen's eyes widened. "Welsh?"

"Uh-huh. Pastry chef from Anglesey. Lives in Paris now."

"Really?" Owen replied, assessing her carefully.

She looked like she'd recognised him when he walked in. Now it made sense. She probably followed the rugby.

"She's come over to help Beth out for a while. It's real good of her and it's given us some family time."

Gareth studied his brother. So, Owen was into Alys.

"I need to tell you something," Rhys cut across. He had them all around and the incident had been bothering him for days.

"A few nights ago, Adam and his pals made an appearance here. Doing coke and dealing out of the car park."

Gareth's face became stony. "Does Beth know?"

"Uh-huh. We had a quiet word with them outside and banned them. Thing is, we didn't want to worry Beth, but he made a threat," Rhys filled them in.

"What kind of threat?" Madog asked.

"To burn the restaurant," Rhys said quietly.

"He's in the rugby club with you isn't he?"

The brothers looked at Gareth.

"Yeah. I'll fucking deck him if he comes near here or Beth."

"I'm sure he was just sounding off," Rhys tried to reassure him, "But best take precautions. Check the insurance and put up some cameras outside."

"I think you need a quiet word with the cops too," Owen advised.

Their main course arrived, and they began to eat.

"How's things with Ariana?" Madog asked, nudging Rhys, who nearly choked on his drink.

Like Owen, Rhys was drinking a sparkling water. He gazed out of the window at the sea. Everyone seemed to know he liked her. What did he expect? This was Freshwater Bay. But he sure needed some advice right now. He took a deep breath and looked at his three brothers.

"It's not going too well. There's a slight hiccup."

He explained how he'd been chatting to her online as Luc and how she'd blown him out, telling him that she was in love with Luc so she couldn't go out with him.

"Shit bro! So you've been dumped for your own online alter ego?" Madog puzzled.

"Seems so."

Rhys hung his head and winced as he waited and then saw their reactions, which as predicted came in thick and fast.

"Why can't you ever do things straightforward, Rhys?" Gareth said amazed and amused.

Rhys widened his eyes at his brother. Seriously, was *he* going to lecture *him?*

"Err... who married Beth as *a business arrangement*?"

Gareth grinned, "'Kay, point taken."

"So, the thing is," Rhys continued. "She was about to blow her dosh on a plane ticket to Los Angeles, so I had to improvise quickly. I've arranged for Luc to meet her next week in Cardiff. Not sure how to play it yet. What d'you think I should do?"

Rhys looked around at them as the brothers sat in silence, staring at him. He grimaced and they all erupted into peals of infectious laughter.

"What! So you're both going to Cardiff to meet each other as Luc and Bianca?" Owen chuckled, calming down.

Rhys put his cutlery down, sat back and rubbed his hand over the back of his neck.

"Yeah man, I know, it's totally fucked up. I may need to stay at yours if it all goes pear-shaped, which knowing my luck, it will."

"No worries, bro."

Owen shook his head in disbelief at his brother.

"I'd give good money to watch you two meet. Ariana is going to be so pissed!" Madog sighed, recovering from laughing so hard.

"You *think*?" Rhys groaned at his predicament.

His brothers were still laughing at him as the waitress cleared their plates and brought them the dessert menu.

"Holy shit! This dessert is exceptional. If the nutritionist even gets a sniff that I'm eating this, I'm off the team."

Owen gave an orgasmic groan as he tasted the rich bitter chocolate ganache with a light chocolate and honeycomb mousse.

"Whoever made this is an angel."

"An Anglesey angel," ribbed Gareth.

Owen put his spoon down and his eyes once again raked over the girl he'd been studying all meal.

"Really?"

Those curves were in all the right places, he thought to himself as he appreciated the pudding and the creator afresh.

Gareth nodded, smiling.

"I'm marrying that woman."

There was an intent and purpose to his proclamation. And when Owen wanted something, he always got it.

After lunch, Gareth said farewell to his brothers before heading back to the boathouse.

"Don't forget, Thursday night, five thirty, at the village hall. It's ready to load but bring your tools, just in case," Rhys reminded him.

Gareth had agreed to move the set and help out at the drama competition. Rhys was a natural with those kids, Dan was buzzing about him.

"No worries. Be glad to get out. Beth's having the girls round," he winked, clasping Rhys' shoulder as he left.

Madog gave Owen a brotherly punch. He needed to get back too, for milking.

"Apart from your dramatic love life, how you doing?" Owen asked Rhys as they strolled down the hill back from the restaurant into Freshwater Bay harbour.

"Real good," Rhys reflected. "No uncontrollable urges to drink. Everything's pretty calm. Ariana asked me to be her business partner today."

"What did you say?" Owen asked.

They'd reached the harbour and he moved towards the vacant bench facing out to the boats.

"That I'd think about it," Rhys said, sitting beside him.

"And?"

"I think I'll do it. I enjoy the sales and the web design. That's what I did in America, remember, too. I need something more solid now, you know, help me fund my extravagant actor lifestyle and all. No, seriously,

I should be trying to get a car and a roof over my head that's not my old teacher's garden shed."

Owen nodded, "You could live on the boat?"

Gareth had spent his first few months there when he was renovating the boathouse.

"Nah. That's worse than the shed."

"Gareth asked me to train again with the rugby team, but I don't think that's a good plan. Too much booze and Adam will be there."

Owen agreed. The drinking culture of local club rugby couldn't easily be avoided. Even if he didn't buy drinks for himself, there were the spirit mixes given regularly as dares, unspeakable initiation ceremonies and endless rounds of shots lined up for everyone on the bar. There was no ducking out if you wanted to be in the rugby club. It would be too easy for Rhys to regress.

"Steer well clear, Rhys," Owen advised sagely.

CHAPTER TWELVE

"*Oh My God!* Why didn't anyone tell me that Owen Morgan, rugby *legend*, is Gareth's brother!" Alys exclaimed, looking around at Ariana and Rhian sat on the sofa, and at Beth who was nursing Finn.

They were nearly through their second bottle of Prosecco, even with Beth and Rhian not drinking. Ariana had invited her best mate Rhian along because she thought it would be good for Beth to get to know someone else with young kids and a baby on the way.

"Is it a defence to say, you didn't ask?" Beth shrugged.

"I made such a fool of myself. He came in, *Geez, Louise!* He's a six five muscle man. All I could do was talk to his chest."

Alys pulled a pained face and drank some more bubbles.

All he could do was look at your chest too, all the way through lunch, Beth thought. Gareth had told her everything, but she couldn't tell Alys. Firstly, because she'd never believe her, and secondly, because she was feeling split loyalties on this one, and decided it was best to keep schtum. Gareth would never tell her anything if she blabbed, and Owen was too well known for her to gossip. Plus, he had a famous girlfriend. They were often snapped together at socials and coming out of clubs for the tabloid news.

Owen had *certainly* noticed Alys' assets. She was blessed with an hourglass figure and long, thick, smooth auburn hair. Problem was, Alys always seemed to think she was fat, and it made her have serious insecurities when it came to men. It was absolutely ridiculous, of course, but there was no shifting her low self-esteem. She'd spent all the service, according to Gareth, working by the door or at the pass, assiduously avoiding them. He told Beth that Owen had tried to get to talk to her, to tell her how amazing her chocolate mousse was, but that she'd ducked into the back kitchen before he got the chance.

The bubbles were flowing, and the girls were giggling. Beth told Rhian the story of how she met Gareth and how she came to inherit La Galloise. Rhian told them about her childhood sweetheart Will and how they got married young. Will did a lot with the rugby club and Beth had seen him once or twice when she'd gone to a social event with Gareth.

"Adam sends his regards." Rhian nudged Ariana.

"He can stick his regards up his arse," Ariana snorted.

Beth's eyes widened.

"I went out with him once. Big mistake. He's a total knobhead," Ariana said by way of explanation and studied her glass.

"Thought you said Rhys was a dick too?" Beth reminded her.

"This guy makes Rhys look like an angel, believe me. He was Rhys' best mate in school. Very bad news," Ariana replied.

Beth agreed, he was someone she never wanted to see at La Galloise again. They'd had a confidential meeting with the Police earlier to raise their concerns about the drugs and the threat Adam had made. She noted Ariana's bitter tone and changed the topic.

"Things hotting up with Mr Morgan, then? Heard he's living in your garden now," she quipped.

"You wouldn't believe me if I told you."

Ariana looked at them conspiratorially. She'd been dying to tell them.

"Try us," Alys egged her on.

"Fine. But you've got to swear to keep this a secret. No spillages. Swear?"

They did and she told them the sorry tale of Luc. How they'd met, how it had progressed and how she found out it was, in fact, Rhys all along. She didn't tell them about Rhys' addictions, but *what she did want* was some advice on was how she should handle the Cardiff meeting in a few days' time.

"So, let's recap... He doesn't know you know... You've been giving him the cold shoulder, and now you're both going to get to Cardiff *and*..." Rhian was trying to fill in the gaps of this twisted tale. Beth and Alys were trying to catch up.

"*And*, I need to teach the boy a lesson," Ariana told them decisively.

"He's a *bugger* but you're still into him, *right*?" Alys asked.

Ariana flushed and they all giggled some more.

"*So*...," Rhian pursued.

"*So*... I'm a bit stuck on what to do next," Ariana admitted.

"This is your idea so far, yeah?... You meet in a city bar."

Rhian acted it out with her hands as shadow puppets, her fingers and thumbs becoming talking mouths.

"Hey Bianca, you look *a lot* like this girl I know, called Ariana... Luc, *shit*, you look *identical* to my ex-boyfriend, Rhys... *Duh!*... We've both so *stoopid*... kiss... kiss."

Alys and Beth roared with laughter, watching Ariana suck it up.

"Why don't you say you're shy?" Alys began as the laughing died down a little.

"Once, I made Gareth wear a blindfold."

Everyone turned in surprise at Beth sharing her secrets.

"*Hey!* It was very sexy actually. He was really turned on by it."

She coloured up and fussed over Finn.

Ariana's brain worked over the ideas. What if she did insist that they meet in the dark in a hotel room? The idea made her heart go faster. She needed to think about this some more.

Dan took the trophy as the whole group came up onto the stage. The crowd clapped exuberantly, and Rhys winked at Dan as he turned to look for him in the wings. They'd gone and done it. He was proud of every single one of them. They'd worked their butts off for the last two weeks and it had paid off. Even little Mai had nailed it. She'd been so frightened before she went out, that he had to do some breathing with her to calm her down. There was no doubt though that Aled, who played the grumpy dairy farmer lead, was the star of the show. But he was only as good as the others who were feeding him and reacting to his lines. That boy would go far. Rhys would have a word with him after about what he wanted to do. He could do more than just amateur dramatics if he wanted to, he thought.

Gareth helped Rhys and the boys load the set back into the pickup to store at the farm. They were through to the national competition and would be doing it all again in July.

"How does it feel being back on the boards?" Gareth asked his brother.

He was still curious about why he was back but had let him settle, he didn't want to push it.

"It was nice being in the wings instead of on stage," Rhys answered pensively, "I'm so proud of those guys. They were on fire tonight."

"You going back to it soon?"

Gareth got into the truck beside Rhys and put on his seat belt.

"Maybe. But not back to The States."

There was silence as Gareth sat beside him. He hadn't started the engine, somehow sensing that Rhys wanted to talk.

"Gareth, this isn't a public announcement, so no blabbing, but I've recently come out of rehab. I've been over two months sober and clean."

Gareth turned his head to look at his brother.

"*Jees* Rhys, why didn't you say?"

He thought about it for a second.

"*Shit!* You're working the bar. Why didn't you *tell* us?"

"Working the bar's not a problem. There's no temptation there. My triggers are stressors and mental health. L.A. depressed the shit out of me. All the blags of being an actor."

"Be honest, Rhys. You've had a problem for years. Those of us who knew were always worried about all the drugs you were taking."

"Yeah. I s'pose."

Gareth started the engine and began reversing out of the space.

"Well, you're looking much better these days, not so thin, even if you *have* lost your California suntan."

Gareth was quiet taking in the information.

"*Jesus, Rhys!* You alright now?"

"Since I've been home, I've been so much better, man."

He gave Gareth's shoulder a friendly punch.

"I thought *that* was maybe down to the influence of a certain *jewellery designer.*"

"Yeah that too," Rhys agreed and ventured, "These guys tonight and what they achieved. That's what it's all about, yeah?"

Gareth smiled in agreement. Dan told him how Rhys had worked with them and turned the play around.

They drove quietly for a few minutes as Gareth seemed to be wrestling with what to say.

"You got lost for a bit but it's great to have you back with us, Rhys," he said finally.

Rhys nodded, "I'm home and it feels good. Now it's time for me to get my shit together."

Luc: You all set for Wednesday?

Ariana was online. She'd been watching out for his return. She'd been dying to find out how the kids got on in their drama competition but there was no way she could do that now. The light was on in the studio and he was online too.

Bianca: Yes. I'll be there. 7.30 The Singing Canary. You got a place to stay?

She'd chosen a pub to meet at not far from the station, she'd not booked a hotel room, but she'd wing that one. She'd take overnight stuff in a big slouch bag and go online and find a room last minute if she needed to.

Luc: I'm booked into Hotel Violet. You know it?

Bianca: No, sorry. How's London?

Luc: Cold. Wet. I miss the L.A. sunshine

How long was he going to keep up this pretence? She gazed down at the window of the studio. Liar, liar, pants on fire, she thought.

Bianca: You don't know how much I'm looking forward to meeting you finally, Luc. How will I know you?

Here we go, red rose, copy of the Cardiff Echo. What was he going to suggest? There was a pause, then he typed.

Luc: Easy. I'll know you. You'll be the most beautiful girl in the bar. And we'll be wearing our rings

Smooth, very smooth, Rhys Morgan. She wanted to play with him for a while longer.

Bianca: But, honestly now, what if we don't like what we see? Luc, I'm worried cos we've never seen what we look like. What if I'm not attracted to you? If you're not attracted to me?

Luc: I'll be coming through the door at 7.30 sharp. Check it's me. Look for the Claddagh ring. If you don't like what you see, you can walk away

She reread his response. He knew she was going to find out it was him and that knowing Rhys, he predicted that she'd just melt into his arms at the sight of him when he made his grand entrance. He presumed, cockily, she thought, that this was in the bag. Smug bastard. She was going to teach him a little life lesson, she decided.

Bianca: So excited to finally be meeting you. Keep online in case of any problems

Luc: Will do. Sweet dreams Bianca xx

Ariana was squealed with delight when Rhys told her that he was going to take her up on her offer. They were walking along the cliff tops the next morning to the gallery. They had unconsciously taken each other's hands as they walked, her fingers threaded through his, although nothing else had happened between them since she'd declared her unswerving love for Luc. He'd been the perfect gentleman, he thought, amused. He'd also booked a Cardiff hotel room for Wednesday night that week. He was an optimist. She'd show up in the bar, where they'd arranged to meet. He'd explain Luc away and he'd convinced himself that she'd forgive him. He'd leave out the small matter of the five thousand pounds. Best bury that guilty secret. What could go wrong, he thought to himself? She might fly off the handle, but he was confident he could bring her around. They were business partners now, after all, he grinned to himself.

David opened the heavy oak door into the gallery mid-morning. He'd come to pick Rhys up; they were going to see a car that Rhys had found online.

"Hi, Mr Morgan."

Ariana straightened up from leaning over Rhys who was at his laptop.

"David, please," he told her as he walked over to them.

His eyes roved around the space in wonder. He'd not been in the gallery since he'd bought Ellen a ring a few years back. He was amazed, this time and last, at the diversity of pieces in there and was taken by the large coloured glass chandelier hanging from the ceiling.

"Come and see what Rhys has created," Ariana motioned for him to come over.

David joined them at the computer, as Rhys took him through the new website and the linked sites and marketplaces.

"Meet my new business partner," Ariana told David proudly.

"I don't mind admitting that he's turned this business around."

"You've done this?" David said incredulously as he was guided through the slick websites.

He suddenly realised that he didn't know his son at all.

"So, you're sticking around?"

David was driving, with Rhys sitting alongside in the front of his Land Rover Discovery.

"Uh-huh. I really enjoy doing the web design and I get a buzz when we make a sale, but I've been thinking about something else too."

He wanted to test it out on his dad.

"I've been toying with the idea of going into teaching."

"Teaching?"

David raised an eyebrow. He'd had more calls home from school about Rhys than all of the other boys put together.

"Poacher turned gamekeeper, eh?" David chuckled.

"Yeah, something like that."

Rhys' lips cracked into a smirk; he knew exactly what his dad was thinking about. He'd been a terror in school, and there'd been a few close scrapes with the headteacher.

"Drama, but I could teach English, even Welsh at a push. What d'ya think?"

"Whatever you decide, son, you'll do well. I'm sure of that."

David placed his hand briefly on Rhys' knee.

"Y'think?" Rhys said uncertainly.

"I know. Now stop mucking that Ariana Jones about and tell her how you really feel about her," he tutted, "Business partner, indeed!"

Rhys laughed, "*Hah!* Yeah, well like everything else with me, it's a little complicated right now, but I am working on it."

Rhys had picked out a mid-range black four-wheel-drive car. It was fairly low mileage, good value with a solid service and owner history. David watched as Rhys charmingly beat down the price further with the owner than he would have gone. And he got the deal. Yes, the boy would be fine, he thought. Time to show him something, he decided.

As Rhys took the car keys from the owner, David called to him.

"Follow me back to the farm. I've something I want you to see."

She couldn't concentrate. Rhys had gone off to buy a car with his dad. He'd agreed to be her business partner. What did that mean? He was going to stay, her heart leaped at the thought.

She kept thinking about Wednesday in Cardiff, what was she going to say to him? Was she going to go through with her plan? What was she going to wear?

She closed up the gallery and wandered back through Freshwater Bay to Gwen's cottage. She wasn't going to be able to get *anything* done until she'd sorted her head out and had gone through her wardrobe.

As she walked into the kitchen of the cottage, Ariana stood still and stared at the state of the place. She couldn't believe that one woman could make such a mess in so little time.

When she'd left that morning, the kitchen had been spotless. Now, it was like a mad professor's laboratory. There were jars and lids everywhere. Cooled pools of wax dripped all over the surfaced, puddles of unidentified liquid spillages across the floor and dried pieces of stalks and petals littered the worktops. Label backings were strewn wildly all over the kitchen table, and in the centre of it all, was the master at work.

Gwen Jones, five foot nothing, in an oversized apron, leaning over a Chinese burner and a bubbling cauldron-like skillet. Her glasses were steamed up and she was stirring the pot with a big ladle, mixing her flower oils into the liquid beeswax ready to fill pots of her homemade cosmetics. The acrid air smelled of burned candles.

"Good day at the office, dear? Home a little early aren't we? I will clean it up before Rhys gets back, *cariad*, so don't worry," she teased as Ariana walked into the chaos.

"Not even going there."

Ariana shook her head and went up the stairs to her bedroom. Why couldn't she just make sponge cakes and scones like every other grandma? Why was it she had to have the mad witch version? She laughed to herself. *God!* but she loved Gwen so much. She wouldn't have it any other way.

She started to look through her wardrobe and then her drawers. What did one wear on a blind date with your business partner, she thought? This was *so fucked up,* even she couldn't make this up.

Finally, she found what she had been hunting for. The labels were still attached from when she'd bought them last year. She pulled them out of the store bag and tried them on. The silk of the cami top and knickers felt wonderful on her skin and she knew he'd enjoy the suspender belt. The ivory underwear was full-on vintage with a Forties French feel to it. She loved the appliqued lace detailing on the silk of the v cut triangular cups of the cami top and on the trim of the knickers. She looked at the delicate, seamed stockings still in the pack. She'd save those for Wednesday.

Looking through her wardrobe, she chose a tight red pencil skirt with a back slit and a black silk blouse with a relaxed reeve neck. She teamed it up with a black batik patterned scarf she'd made herself, that would double up for what she had in mind. She changed and found her large slouch bag that she used for overnight stays. She folded what she needed into the bag. A pair of jeans and a more casual top, another scarf, a wash bag and toiletries. Dare she put in some condoms? Her pulse raced. She played with the Claddagh ring on her finger. The anticipation of finally being with Rhys thrilled her. It was going to be a long two days to wait.

Rhys parked up behind David. They'd passed the farmhouse and David had driven up the road to the fields beyond the farmhouse. They got out by a grassed-over track that would take them eventually out over towards the cliff tops and the sea.

"Talk a walk with me," David told him, and they began strolling casually down the track together.

Rhys hadn't been down here for years, he realised. That showed how much he'd avoided helping out on the farm, he thought a tad guiltily. He'd forgotten about this place. David led him further down the lane to a hollow. There was a stream running through the meadow here, and a wonderful mature oak tree that must have been a few centuries old. The verdant ground was covered in lush spring grass and primroses, and the hedgerows around it were bursting with all the beautiful spring flowers, yellow celandines, the blues of speedwell and forget-me-nots and peppered white sprays of stitchwort. The bluebells were just starting to flower. The ground would soon be a spectacular carpet of lilac-blue, Rhys thought. The hollow was sheltered from the weather and in the corner at the back of the field was a tumble-down building, an old stone farmhouse, derelict with a hole in the roof. A crow cawed at them from the chimney pot, jealously guarding his new spring home.

"It's yours if you want it, son."

David looked at Rhys.

"Not much, I know. It's a project. But we'll all help you out."

Rhys stood transfixed. The path continued from the house up to the cliffs and then down to the sea. He turned to his father, a little overcome by his father's generous offer. He coughed and cleared the lump that had formed in his throat.

"It's perfect," he said.

CHAPTER THIRTEEN

Gwen dropped Ariana at the train station, and they said goodbye briskly since a parking warden had spotted her as she pulled into the drop off zone. She watched Ariana go into the station through her rear-view mirror as she put on the car's indicators to re-join the traffic. Ariana hadn't explained where she was going, more than a vague 'see a man about a dog' type excuse. Rhys had also gone off in his new car, the day before, to see his brother Owen in Cardiff. It was going to be a quiet couple of days.

Gwen rubbed her throat automatically and reached over to the cubby hole by the gear stick. Her free hand rattled through the loose change, as she drove through the traffic until she found the pack of antacid tablets she'd been searching for. She popped one out of the blister pack and let it melt on her tongue as she waited at the traffic lights.

Ariana arrived at Cardiff station a little after seven. She knew Rhys had been staying overnight at Owen's and she guessed that he'd been kicking his heels all day. Her face lit up as she thought about how psyched he'd be about this date. He was probably pacing now, waiting for seven thirty to arrive. He hoped he was as nervous as she was. He had, after all, more to lose, wondering how she was going to react when she found out the truth.

She walked from the station up to the main shopping area and centre of the city and, using her phone, found and then plonked herself out of the way at a trendy coffee shop opposite the Singing Canary. Hotel Violet was a ten-minute walk away. She knew where that was now. She ordered an espresso and sat in the corner by the window. She smoothed out her tight pencil skirt, hoped her stocking seams were straight and waited for Rhys to arrive and go into the bar opposite.

He didn't disappoint. He sloped into view at exactly seven twenty-five, looking edgy and a little shifty. He was wearing an open-necked black shirt she'd not seen before and light-coloured jeans with converse type trainers. And, she noticed; he was wearing the ring. He looked hot, she thought and took a deep breath to calm her nerves. She would give him ten more minutes to sweat on it before she'd get in touch.

Rhys edged into the bar and looked around. He'd been waiting all day for this moment and he was antsy and anxious. The place was poorly lit

111

and full of dark corners; leather chesterfields and speakeasy booths, tucked away for private liaisons, he thought. He ordered a coke from a bored-looking bartender and casually made his way round the empty spaces, searching for Ariana. It was a quarter to eight by now and he still couldn't see her. *Shit!* Did this mean that she'd spotted him and walked away? Was this the end of it all? It meant he wouldn't be able to talk her around.

His phone pinged. She had sent him a message.

Bianca: Sorry Luc, feeling super nervous about this. Can I make a new place to meet?

Ok, she'd gotten spooked. He breathed a deep breath. Typical Ariana. She'd be anxious like him. Of course.

Luc: Sure, no problem. Don't be scared, Bianca. You know me better than you think

He was giving her a clue.

Bianca: I think I need to get used to you first. You willing to indulge me?

Luc: Whatever you want, Bianca

Bianca: I'm still worried about whether we'll be attracted to each other. Can we meet somewhere more discreet?

Luc: Sure. Your call

Bianca: Your hotel room?

Luc: You sure?

Bianca: Yes. Room number?

Luc: 419

Bianca: OK, Luc, I don't want us to see each other yet

Luc: What do you mean?

Bianca: I want to feel you first. See if I like you. Close the curtains, switch off the light, and....

Luc: Yes?

Bianca: I want you to wear a blindfold. I've left a scarf for you on the coffee shop table across from the Canary. Pick it up and I'll see you at 8.30

He rushed out of the pub to the cafe. She wasn't there. On the table lay a black tie-dyed scarf. He shoved it in his pocket and jogged back to the hotel.

What game was she playing? It was exciting, he had to admit it. His heart was thumping as he closed the curtains and shut out all the light. It was pitch black without the lights on. He quickly tidied his stuff up, brushed his teeth and waited for Ariana. The scarf lay on the bed beside him. He thought about the last time they'd been together. His gut twisted and he hoped she wouldn't tie him up again.

Ariana could barely hold it together. She'd just managed to stay hidden around the corner as Rhys had come rushing out of the pub. She hadn't expected him to be so fast. She'd followed him at a distance and saw him go into the hotel, slipping quietly into the hotel lobby toilets after him where she was busy composing herself, trying to steady her frazzled nerves. Staring into the mirror, she fixed her red lipstick and checked her hair. She'd done it up at the top, curling down her back, like she'd worn it at the Prom all those years ago. She hoped this time, things would work out better between them.

The ride in the elevator seemed the longest of her life as she watched the numbers light up through the floors. It stopped on the second floor and a couple got in to go to the reception, even though she was going up. When the doors finally pinged open, she walked the long corridor to 419 hardly able to breathe. She stopped outside the door and found the other scarf at the top of her bag. With her heart in her mouth, she tied it around her eyes and knocked on the door.

Rhys heard her at the door. He put on his blindfold and felt his way towards it.

"You wearing your blindfold?" she spoke into the door.

Dammit! He was going to have to pretend he was Luc now. He hadn't thought about that.

"Yeah, baby. Come on in."

He slipped effortlessly into a Californian accent, and with some fumbling, opened the door.

She felt her way two steps and bumped into him. She giggled nervously; this wasn't as sexy as she'd imagined it.

"Sorry about this, but I'm so shy and so unsure. I figured that this would be a good first step for us both."

"A little unorthodox, but great to meet you, Bianca."

He found her hand and took it. He was now in role.

"Errr... let's sit if we can move without falling over."

He guided her to sit beside him on the lower edge of the bed.

"It's Ariana."

"Uh?"

113

"My name. It's Ariana. Bianca's my middle name."

"Oh! Okay… Ariana it is."

They sat side by side for a minute, neither knowing what to say.

Ariana felt a little stupid. Was this blindfold idea going to work? And how long was Rhys going to keep up the American accent, she wondered? She needed to move things along a little. He was being very well behaved, a little too well behaved for Rhys, she thought, amused. She'd let him know that she'd busted him in a bit, but she wanted him to enjoy the touch of her first.

"Can I feel what you look like?" she ventured turning to him feeling his heart thump as hers raced too.

Was she right? Was he nervous? The electricity fizzed between them as she swivelled around and placed her hand, first on his shoulder, and then up gently to his face.

She touched his cheek lightly, "I've been dreaming of touching you," she said softly.

He sensed her; he could feel where she was, her breath up close to him, the air crackling with the tension he knew she felt too. Her fingers inched across his face. He leaned into her and found her lips with his, making her pulse quicken. She shuddered as she felt his mouth covering hers; deepening the kiss feverishly, the pent-up energy between them finally finding a release as their tongues tangled and duelled in undisguised fervid, raw lust.

"Wooh, Luc. That was some kiss," Ariana whispered breathlessly, finally pulling apart.

"I knew we'd get along," Rhys replied in a Yankie drawl.

Ariana screwed her nose up battling back a laugh. Rotter.

"Now my turn to feel you," he said huskily.

She moved and stood up tall from the bed, taking his hand. He stood square to her and slowly worked his hands over her. First, he touched her hair.

"Let me guess... long hair. Is it dark?"

He ran his fingers through her long tresses, feeling the silky lengths.

"It is."

He covered his lips over her sweeping neck, caressing her as she leaned her head sidewards, so he had more skin to explore. God, that was good. He moved his hands then down over her soft blouse, towards her breasts. She breathed raggedly as she felt him lingering at a button.

"May I?"

"Yes," she answered quietly as he slowly loosened her blouse following his fingers with kisses down her chest until he could feel the silk of her camisole top and her breasts wrapped up underneath.

"God, *Ariana*, what are you wearing? I need to *see* this," his accent slipping a little as he forgot himself, lost in lustful desire for her.

She smiled secretly.

"Shhh. Just feel."

She found his face with her hand and guided it back to hers, putting her lips to his mouth seductively.

He pulled away slightly.

"May I take off your blouse and…" his hand brushed over her hips and felt the shape of her round butt in the tight pencil. "Your skirt?"

"Yes, you may."

She could hardly speak as she was overwhelmed by the electricity of his touch over her. Her pulse raced as he slowly and deliciously peeled off her blouse and unhooked her skirt. The clothes dropped onto the floor and she discreetly stepped out of the skirt, kicked off her heels and led him back towards the bottom of the bed, where she guided him to lie beside her. His hands oriented themselves, feeling all over her, touching her; gliding over her breasts, her belly, down to her thighs and up to her core, driving her wild with anticipation. Flames of desire licked through her. She wanted him on her, kissing her all over, but she sensed something holding him back. His touch had become more tentative, more unsure.

"Ariana. You sure you want to do this?"

Rhys' fingers grazed the silk of her underwear, caressing her body as she lay on her side beside him. Lace edging and... *Holy Mother of God!* Were those stockings? His fingers stroked over the inside of her thigh and played with the suspender straps.

He had to stop this now or there'd be no going back. Try as he might, he couldn't square himself with the guilt he knew he'd feel of having sex with her under these false pretences.

His voice rasped with passion, "Ariana. I can't do this. Not like this."

He freed himself from her and sat up on the edge of the bed.

"*Rhys Morgan,* just shut up and make love to me, why don't you?"

Ariana tugged the scarf off her eyes and looked at him straight in the darkness. She reached for a sidelight and switched it on.

"You knew!"

He stared at her, dumbfounded, taking his blindfold off too, his eyes adjusting to see her.

"*Duh!* Course I did," Ariana laughed, his face was a picture.

"Ariana, I love you."

The words tumbled out, but he wasn't sorry. He meant it with all his heart.

"I know that, too. Rhys, I want you so badly. I've been waiting a long time for you. *Like ten years*."

She held his hand, examining the Claddagh ring he wore.

"It fits you. I wasn't sure."

"I wore it every day, 'til I came home, and I won't take it off again."

She kissed the ring and pushed him back down on the bed, moving herself on top of him.

"You are so beautiful, Ariana, leave the light on. I want to see you. All of you. Including these suspenders."

"I want to see you too. Now, are you gonna finish what you started here?"

He flashed her an alluring sexy smile.

"I certainly am, Miss Jones."

She unbuttoned his shirt and moved her mouth onto his chest, teasing him with her tongue. He was on fire for her as she eased his jeans down and stripped him to his underwear. He reached for a condom from his trouser pocket and then began exploring her wondrous underwear and those stockings again.

"Did I tell you how much I love these?"

He broke into a broad grin as he opened each suspender popper with this fingers and teeth, moving his mouth to carefully roll down each stocking.

He stripped her slowly and took them on a journey of discovery as he caressed her expertly with his tongue. She felt the waves building up inside her until she could take it no more; she clenched as she saw stars, coming hard for the first time.

She pivoted herself to face him as they lay on their sides and her hand drifted down to free him from his underwear. She rolled him onto his back as she pulled them down, her eyes taking all of him in. How could she forget? She began to work her way down, putting her lips around him and caressing him with the tip of her tongue. He threw his head back and exhaling, gently edged her back up, onto her back, and putting the condom on.

"Ari, *cariad*, I want you like this. Is that okay?" he asked her, gazing into her eyes.

She nodded and he entered her in a long, sweeping thrust, both of them gasping as he filled all of her for the first time. Slowly he began to move inside her, building rhythmically, in measured strokes with her, as she matched him. Harder and deeper, harder and deeper, all the time moving those delicious hands of his on the bundle of nerves that would rocket her skywards. Their sweat covered their bodies, the pace building until finally, she could resist no longer. She clenched, feeling the power of her orgasm over-take her again; this time harder than ever before, she shuddered in ecstasy as she came. He paused and then pushed into her hard, hitting spots she didn't know she had, sending her back over again before she felt him pulsing finally within her, his body quaking too, in spasms of bliss. They both finally collapsed together, boneless, sated.

Neither of them could speak. Rhys wiped away a tear that had escaped and rolled down Ariana's cheek. He kissed it and then kissed her gently, tenderly on the lips.

"No one has ever made me feel like this. I never knew it could be this good," she murmured.

"Me either. It's only ever been *you* I love, Ariana."

Her face melted into a broad smile and she kissed him back. "I love you too, Luc."

She slid her finger across his lips, leaving it lingering there.

"But ever lie to me again and we're done, understand?"

"Yes," he vowed.

His gut twisted, as he left the little problem of the five thousand pounds of stock he'd stolen from her, locked deeply away in his guilty conscience.

Ariana's ringtone pierced the dark silence of the bedroom at three am. They'd been asleep for around an hour. Ariana stirred, her lips were sore from kissing and her legs ached from all the sex they'd had, on the bed, in the shower, on the bed again. Phew. He was a machine, she grinned, as she moved over him to find her bag and grab the phone. Rhys moved. It was Gwen.

"Hello?" she croaked, answering.

"Is that Ariana Jones?"

It was a male voice; it was kind but sounded like he meant business.

"Yes?"

"I'm Gary. I'm a paramedic. I'm here with Gwen. She's had a heart attack and we're in the ambulance. Can you get over to the hospital in Holyguard? Come through A&E."

"Is she okay?"

Ariana took in all the details. Gwen was being rushed into surgery. Rhys was awake and picking up fragments of the call. He knew that something was wrong and so grabbed his clothes and got dressed hastily. Ariana rushed into his arms as the call ended.

"Gwen's had a heart attack. We need to get back."

Rhys held her close to him for a moment as she let out an involuntary sob. He held her face and looked into her eyes.

"*Cariad*, she's in good hands now. My car's at Owen's in the Bay. I'll call a taxi to drive us over. Once we get going, we should get there from Cardiff in two hours or so."

He ordered the taxi immediately, as Ariana dressed into her jeans and got ready to leave.

CHAPTER FOURTEEN

"Please God, please make her come through this."

Ariana prayed silently as she sat in a visitor area on the post-operative ward, waiting for Gwen to come out of surgery. It was nearly dawn and they'd not had any word about her since they'd been guided to the room to wait. Rhys rubbed his eyes, stretched out around Ariana as they sat on the hard chairs, waiting. He was so tired, even his bones were aching.

"Why?"

The question hung on Ariana's lips as she waited in the empty room.

"Why what?" Rhys said sleepily.

"Why did you feel the need to be Luc, to pretend to be someone else?"

"Would you have talked to me if I'd got in touch as Rhys?"

"Probably not."

"It's was the only thing I could think to do at the time. Get into character."

"I'm kinda glad you did," Ariana said giving his trainer a friendly kick.

"Why didn't you hate me after what I did to you? I know you had to live with them calling you Rhys the Cock."

Rhys humphed. They had, but not to his face or he'd have floored them.

"I did, for quite a while," he said truthfully and paused while he considered it further.

"Ariana Jones, you're the only one who's ever given me what I deserved. You started out as a challenge, and you turned into my best friend. You even saved me from myself when I was in my darkest place."

Ariana thought about that.

"Hmm, I just wish I'd known it was you. I could have helped you more."

She tried to lighten the mood.

"Did you know about the Rhys Morgan cock and balls pinata at the rugby club?"

"Oh yes. What can I say? At least they made it big," Rhys said wryly.

"I'm sorry Rhys for what I did. You pissed me off with that camera, but I should've just walked away. It was really wrong of me to take that pic and post it online."

He dropped a light caress on the top of her head.

119

"Don't worry, Miss Jones, you're long forgiven."

"I am?" she smiled coyly.

"You know you are, but if you do feel the need to grovel, I can think of a few more ways you can make it up to me."

He whispered them into her ear.

"Rhys Morgan!" she exclaimed in mock outrage, giggling.

"Hey! You're the one who started the kinky stuff when you tied me up. Been thinking about it ever since."

Finally, as the ward next door was coming to life with patients having breakfast and nurses doing their first morning rounds of tests, a gurney rolled past their waiting room. Ariana went to the door to look and saw the tiny frame of Gwen on it, unconscious with tubes and drips attached. She was put into a side ward and a nurse let them know that they could sit with her while she came round from the anaesthetic from her triple bypass surgery. Rhys went to get them some coffee as Ariana sat holding Gwen's hand as she came to.

It was midday by the time Gwen was fully conscious. She was still sedated and hooked up to all manner of tubes, drips, drains and monitors, but she was able to speak a little.

"Oh Gran, I was so worried about you."

Ariana kissed her forehead.

"I'm a tough old bird, this is just a blip," Gwen tried to reassure her but spoke weakly.

"Thank you both for being here for me."

She held both her hands out to them, and Rhys and Ariana each held one.

"Ah, my two favourites," she smiled at them serenely and promptly told them to go home, she needed a little rest.

"And if I pop it, remember Ed's promised me twenty-five percent friends and family discount on the funeral," she murmured, trying to reassure them with a joke.

It had the opposite effect, unfortunately, and Rhys had to comfort Ariana, who was already hanging on by an emotional thread.

Leaving Ariana's mobile phone details with the nurses at the desk, they left the hospital and Rhys drove back them back to Freshwater Bay. At the cottage, she led him to her room, and they undressed and slept in each other's arms, exhausted.

By the time they returned to the hospital for visiting hours that evening, Gwen was less groggy. She had more colour and had eaten a light tea. She was trying to sit up and was starting to give them instructions of all the things she needed them to do. All good signs, Ariana thought. The ward sister told them that Gwen would be in for a week, and they would need help for a couple of months, while she recovered at home. Ariana had phoned her mother and father, and they were on their way from Ireland.

In the car on the way home, Ariana was quiet.

"What you thinking about?" Rhys asked her.

"Hmm. Hell of a twenty-four hours," Ariana answered.

Rhys agreed.

"What now?"

"I want food and then you in my bed again."

Ariana put her hand on his thigh as he drove.

"I'll need the studio for a few days for my parents if it's okay with you?"

Rhys nodded and looked at Ariana in the passenger seat.

"I'll be wherever you are. I'm just grateful you didn't buy a plane ticket to LAX."

She giggled, " I *totally* knew who you were, *Rhys Morgan.*"

"You did?"

"*Oh yes!* Taming of the Shrew, remember. Bianca and Lucentio."

"You got me," Rhys smirked, "So... that night, when you said you were in love with Luc?"

She grinned, "Your face was a picture."

He shook his head and laughed.

"Heartless and cruel, Miss Jones. Leaving me in a very uncomfortable state of affairs. Just you wait 'til I get you home."

Ariana raised an eyebrow and flashed him a look that had him pressing his foot down even harder on the accelerator.

"My body's out of whack. I feel jet-lagged," Ariana complained as she sat at the kitchen table. They had both wolfed down the full plate of steak, salad and chips they'd made.

Rhys knew that feeling well.

"How 'bout a coffee? At our favourite spot."

They took their drinks outside and walked down to the driftwood log by the sea. It was May now and the air was warmer but still edged with a little chill. They sat with their mugs, looking out at the waves. Rhys had grabbed a throw and wrapped it around Ariana, drawing her into him. He was never letting her go, he thought to himself. The moon was out, and the cove sparkled in the monochrome light.

"Ari?"

"Hmm."

"Can I take you for a drive?"

"So we can make out?"

"I wanna show you something."

He drove her through Freshwater Bay, past his parents farm, further on, pulling up on the side of the road by a grassy track. He got out of the car, opened the door for her and took her by the hand, fingers weaved together as they walked in the eerie night light down the lane, towards the sheltered grassy hollow. An owl screeched from the woodland behind them, breaking the silence.

"Where you taking me, Rhys?" Ariana asked, intrigued.

"You'll see."

He stopped. There, beside the track, was a meadow covered in bluebells, silvery in the moonlight. And in the corner of it sat an old, tumbledown farmhouse.

"Dad's given this to me. It's a wreck, but what do you think?"

Ariana walked into the middle of the sea of bluebells and stood looking at the cottage in the grey silvery night.

"Would you come live here with me, Ariana? Make this our home. I love you so much it hurts."

She knelt and pulled him down onto the bluebells with her.

"I love you too, Rhys. Yes."

They kissed hot and feverishly, tangling together wildly, ravenously, recklessly, until he finally took her in the lush grassy meadow, their glistening naked bodies, bathed in moonlight, fusing into one.

"Shit, no condom," he realised as they lay together wasted and breathless, side by side, looking at the stars in the clear sky.

"I'm so sorry, Ariana."

"Hey, I was there too. It's okay. I'm on the pill and have regular checks," she reassured him. Her pill-taking had been a bit hit and miss, but she was sure it'd be fine. She resolved to stick a reminder on her phone about it, as she pulled a piece of grass out from the back of her hair. Thank God it was dark, she thought in her nakedness; they'd need a shower when they got back.

"The treatment clinic tested me for everything too, from crack to the clap," he quipped, kissing her, relieved.

"So, I take it, you like this place?"

They hurriedly picked their discarded clothing off the ground and slipped their clothes back on.

"It's fantastic. Let's go and look in," Ariana replied, excitedly.

It was a little creepy in the dark, and there were a few squawks as they disturbed the resident crows, but Ariana could see beyond that.

"Rhys, there's such potential here. Can you see it too?"

"Probably be better in daylight, but yes. It's perfect for us. I'm sorry if this is too fast for you, Ari, but I know what I want now, and it's to be with you."

"Me too. You think I offer a business partnership to anyone who walks in off the street with a few fancy web skills?"

"Very smart."

He tickled her and she squealed into the night stillness.

"But Rhys, how will we afford the renovation?"

"My rainy day account."

She cocked her head.

"The money I made as a kid, and in London. I saved it. The soaps, that God awful hospital drama where I played the young builder who broke his back swinging from the scaffolding. Remember me in that film as the cockney gangster?"

"Ahh yes, and the wizard films," Ariana chipped in.

"The pinnacle of my career, apparently."

He blew onto her neck and started tickling her again.

"I've got a cheap architect and builder too. Gareth will help us, I'm sure."

He paused and stroked her hair, pulling her back to him.

"I'm going to apply for teacher training for the Autumn. What d'you think?"

"I can totally see you doing that. You'll be an amazing teacher," Ariana said running her hand along his jaw.

"But My God!" she snorted.

123

"What?" he exclaimed, laughing at the noise she'd made.

She put her hand to her mouth to control herself.

"In school. You were *so naughty!*"

"Hmm, that's what Dad said too,"

"Ruth the Truth! She never came back after," Ariana reminded him.

He'd locked Miss Ruth Jenkins, the young Religious Education teacher, in the store cupboard at the back of the class. She'd shouted and cried. He viewed it as a victory, back then.

"Not my finest hour," Rhys said regretfully. Two weeks in Mr Morris' naughty kid unit followed. That was where he'd started hanging out with Adam Williams and the boys. Where the rollies had become spliffs.

Laughing and sharing school stories and their plans for the farmhouse, they strolled back to the car, and to bed in the cottage.

The gallery had been closed for a couple of days, and they decided to shut for the week and rearrange their shifts at the restaurant as they cleaned out the studio for Ariana's parents and took daily hour-long drives to visit Gwen in hospital. Paul and Alys worked around it under the circumstances, and it was easier now that there were more chefs trained in bar work. Rhys and Ariana kept an eye on the web sales and spent an hour a day posting out the orders. Ariana also put a call out for more stock. She agreed with Rhys they needed to look at widening their artist pool and think of wholesale options soon.

"Things are going to get even busier here once Gwen comes out of hospital, she'll need us to care for her for a while," he said to Ariana.

"Then, the questions will start flying. About us. Me, here, with you."

Ariana knew that only too well.

"Ahh well," she said, "We're both adults. Gwen won't mind, she'll be pleased for us. Anyway, it'll give them something to talk about. Think we'd better front up to your mother, though. I know Ellen, she'll flip if she hears it second hand."

She clocked Rhys' panicked expression as he shuddered at the truth of this.

"Don't worry, pal," Ariana winked at him cheekily, "Ellen's a pussy cat. Besides, she likes me."

Rhys held his breath as he walked with Ariana into the kitchen of his parents' farm.

"Finally!" David exclaimed as he saw that Rhys was holding Ariana's hand tightly. He slapped Rhys on the back, kissed Ariana on the cheek and went to put the kettle on to the range.

Ellen, coming in from pegging out the washing, beamed when she saw Rhys and Ariana sitting at the table together.

"Well, well!" she said, as she scanned them both, clearly together, "How's Gwen?"

"Getting better, thanks, Ellen," Ariana replied, "Hopefully, she'll be home in a few days, and then she's got a couple of months taking it easy. She's the world's worst patient, and you know she never sits down, so the hard work begins when she gets home."

Ellen nodded in agreement. Gwen and her were friends from way back. "I'll come over, help you sort her out if she's any trouble," she said humorously.

Ariana had no doubt that she would.

"Thanks Ellen."

Rhys squeezed Ariana's hand under the table, she could feel the tension in him as he cleared his throat.

"Actually, there's something else I need to tell you."

Ellen studied Rhys and then Ariana.

"It's about me, and why I came home. You need to know the truth."

Rhys took a deep breath and told them everything. His failed career, the lies he'd told them because of his shame, the drugs and his depression, his loneliness and the drinking.

Tears rolled down his mother's cheeks as he told them all about his night on the bridge and how Ariana had helped him through it all; how unknowingly she'd been there for him when he needed her most. David's eyes shifted from his son to Ariana, and he mouthed her a silent thank you. She nodded in acknowledgement. Ariana felt this was the bravest thing she'd ever seen anyone do.

"Rhys!"

Ellen got out of her chair and went to hug him tight.

"We had no idea."

"It's a relief to tell you," he said finally, through his own tears as his mother clung desperately to him.

He could feel the weight of the lies and his failures lifting from his shoulders. Only one more wrong to put right, he told himself. The trickiest of all.

"Ariana, Owen and Gareth have helped me through this. I wouldn't be here without them," he told them frankly.

David helped his wife regain her composure, and he put his hand on her arm, gesturing for her to let go of her boy now and let him get his breath back.

"Have you seen this boy's work on the computer?" David said to Ellen.

Ariana grinned and got her phone out. Ellen and David hovered around her phone as she swiped through the pages.

"He did this?" Ellen said surprised.

"He's turned my little gallery around, already. Rhys Morgan is more of a businessman than even *he* knows."

Ariana winked at Rhys and David gave his son a gentle pat on the back.

"I've phoned the university. I'm going for an interview next week for teacher training. Hopefully, I can pick up some hours teaching Drama or English," Rhys told them.

"I'm so proud of you, son," Ellen said finally, "More *now*, than *ever* before. Never feel you have to lie to us again. Promise?"

"I promise."

He looked first at his mother and then his father.

"I'm sorry if I've caused you pain. I am trying to be better."

Rhys kissed his mother on the forehead and turned to Ariana.

"Ari, tell them about our plans for the old farmhouse."

Rhys and Ariana picked her parents up from the ferry port. Rhys hadn't met them before, and straight away they were joking and bantering with him like they'd known each other for years. Ariana's mother, Sofia, was very like her daughter to look at; statuesque with long black hair. She fussed over Ariana and looked at Rhys approvingly. She'd finally found herself a very handsome young man, she told her daughter.

When they got to the cottage, Huw, Gwen's son, patted Rhys on the shoulder.

"Right then, boy. Lobster Pot in five minutes?"

Ariana turned to him.

"Actually, Dad, Rhys and I don't drink. I've made some food for us. Why don't we stay here at the cottage, talk properly, before we go see Gwen, eh?"

"*Uhh*, okay. I'm sure we can do that."

Huw pulled a face at his wife, Sofia. This was not how it usually worked. He'd been looking forward to seeing his old friends in the pub.

Ariana looked at him disappointedly. She'd have thought Gwen, rather than the Lobster Pot, would be her father's first priority.

Ariana's parents' visit had been fleeting and perfunctory. Both Ariana and her parents were glad when they were back on the ferry to Ireland. Now Gwen was home, Ariana and Rhys had decided to move into the studio or the 'Shag Shack' as Gwen had now christened it, making both of them go bright red every time she said it. They had thought about staying on in Ariana's room but having considered it further, they decided that the farmhouse project was probably going to take a year or two to build. In the meantime, they needed their own space. The last thing they needed was Gwen embarrassing them further.

So, Ariana was busy painting the shed's lined walls and making better curtains, and Gareth and Rhys were fixing up a small kitchen with some reclaimed units. It would be a bit like camping, they both realised it was basic, but it meant they'd have their own space. It was warm, dry and cosy, Ariana reasoned. Plus, she'd have Rhys here, all to herself. Ariana took to it as a full-on project and was already redesigning the interiors with space-saving ideas from Gareth.

Ellen was over too, making teas and coffees, supplying all Gwen's visitors with cakes and drinks as they came in their droves to visit. It was quite exhausting, but this was a close community and people were concerned and kind. Gwen was lapping up the fuss and held court with Ellen, as their friends gathered each afternoon to see her. Ariana was glad that she'd got a pass on that, but they had enough cake in the freezer to last them a lifetime.

Ariana was amused to see that Ed the Dead, Gwen's undertaker friend, had made a couple of visits to the cottage, each time with a large bunch of flowers. Gwen said he'd tried to see her in the hospital too, but she'd told him not to come. She'd been concerned in case he was measuring her up for that special deal he'd offered her, she joked.

As Rhys relaxed with Ariana into the sofa in the studio that evening, he realised that he was the happiest he'd been in years. But, there was still one huge wrong to put right. He resolved to finish the job now. He needed to transfer the money back to her and tell her about what he'd done to her. He couldn't ask her to share the rest of his life with him living with the final lie that was slowly eating him up a little more each day.

CHAPTER FIFTEEN

Things were getting back to normal as Gwen recuperated from the surgery and Beth was starting to get itchy to get back to work. May was done and the June heat was starting to build. It looked like it was going to be a long, hot summer and the bookings at La Galloise were shaping up nicely.

Alys was in her last week of helping Beth out. She needed to get back to Paris to cover the summer holidays when her boss would be short-staffed. Beth would always be grateful to her friend for coming over, and also to Alys' boss for allowing her the time off. She wrote her a card to thank her and invite her to stay any time at La Galloise. Easing herself back into work, Beth realised just how much she'd missed the place, and with the help of Rhian and Ellen, who babysat when Gareth couldn't have Finn, she was now getting back into her stride.

She sat with Alys on the deck of the boathouse, the June sun made the calm waters glisten all around them, and they looked out across the bay to the uninhabited islands across from them.

"*This is the life*," Alys said, rolling up her jeans and stretching her legs out to catch the sun. "Not a bad view, either."

"Tell me about it," Beth said relaxing into her deck chair with Finn in her arms. "Though I'm not sure what we're gonna do when this little one starts walking. This place is one massive toddler hazard," she said looking at the open deck and all the surrounding seawater.

"Alys, I wanted to fly something by you before you go back. You know how grateful I am, right, for you helping me out like this?" Beth said warmly.

"Yeah 'course. No worries, it's been a pleasure," Alys said, turning her face upwards to the sun to feel the warmth.

"*Umm*, yeah, well, " Beth started.

"The owner of The Lobster Pot's been in touch with me a few times. He's served notice on the tenant there and he's going in a month. I've talked to Gareth and we've decided to take it over."

She paused.

"We're not sure what to do with it yet, but we'd love it if you'd come on board with us into the business. What d'you think?"

"Wow!" Alys was stunned.

"I can't at the moment, Beth, 'cos Celine's given me all this time off and…"

"It wouldn't need to be right away," Beth pacified her, "If you're loving Paris, you could leave in six months, a year, we can even cover for longer. I want to have you with us in this, longer-term."

"Could I bake cakes and bread and sell them?" said Alys, thinking aloud.

"Whatever direction you want to take, we'd talk it through. You'd be with us, helping us to shape the business, take the place forward."

Alys sat quietly, considering it. Freshwater Bay? She'd spent years trying to get out of Wales as a teenager. But while she loved working in the big cities, London, Paris; here, this was a special place, and full of good friends, old and new. They'd become like family to her, already. Maybe, it was time to come home?

"Let me think about it," she said finally, "I can't come back right now, but yes, perhaps in a year."

"Keep it mind, Alys. You know how much I want you here," Beth answered.

She'd planted the seed, she just needed to be patient and let the idea take root and grow.

Ariana and Rhys were back working shifts at La Galloise, and the service had been steady so far that midweek evening.

"You two an item now or what?" Rhys nudged Dan, who was staring across at Lisa talking to customers on table ten, as he poured a pint of lager.

Dan blushed, "Yeah, man."

He added a bottle of cider and a pint glass full of ice beside the pint of lager Rhys had placed on the tray on the bar.

"I thought I saw her at the drama competition."

"Rhys, you know you said I could talk to you…" he said bending over to get a bottle of orange fruit juice out of the drinks fridge.

"Told you, pal. I'm not doing *the talk* with you. Ask yer dad. Just keep those swimmers wrapped up."

Dan tried to flick beer at Rhys' face from a small puddle on the bar top.

"Nah, I wanted to ask you what y'think I should do? Lisa's invited me to the Prom and err… things've been hotting up lately… so I, I went and booked us a room at the hotel. Think she'll like it, or d'ya think she'll go sick?" Dan asked Rhys awkwardly.

"Aww, mate, you've got to tell her first. Don't spring it on her."

Rhys looked at Dan.

"Y' think?"

"I *know*," Rhys said, glancing over at Ariana.

"Hmm."

Dan chewed it over, watching Lisa as she walked by with a stack of plates.

"Take these to nine for me."

He handed Dan the full tray of drinks.

"And remember... no glove, no love," Rhys chuckled as Dan discreetly flipped him the bird with his free hand.

When he had a moment later, Rhys asked Paul quietly if they'd had any more bother with drugs since that night. Apparently, there had been nothing much since, although Paul had intervened and refused to serve Adam and a couple of his chums a few days after. Dan had seen them coming up to the bar, and Paul had been tipped the wink and had intercepted them and got them out of the restaurant with no bother. It was handy having a bit of ex-military muscle around, Rhys thought. Beth was lucky to have him. He'd worked well with Alys and it had given Beth the space she needed for her and Gareth to get used to having little Finn around.

Rhys watched as Ariana worked the restaurant floor. He couldn't wait to get her back home tonight. But how was she going to react when she saw her account balance, he wondered, nervously? There was now fifteen thousand pounds more in it than there had been this morning. It would take her a while to notice, he comforted himself. As a struggling artist, he knew that she'd long had a natural aversion to checking her bank balance.

It was a full five days later when Ariana came rushing over to Rhys with her phone.

"Rhys! Look at this."

Ariana was staring at her bank balance on her phone. Rhys' heart raced and he felt sick. He'd been dreading this moment and had been sweating on it for the full duration of the last five days. He had a rare night off from working either at the restaurant or drama practices with the Young

Farmer group. It was full-on as they were polishing up again for the national competition in July.

He'd been making a pasta Bolognese and there were bubbling pots of pasta and sauce on the small stove they'd put in. He switched them off and went to sit down on the sofa. He patted the sofa beside him, asking her to come and sit with him for a minute. God! How he needed a glass of red wine now. Some courage to get him through this.

"Ari, I need to talk to you."

Ariana noticed the edge in his voice as she went over to him and sat down as he'd asked her to. Something was very wrong.

He inhaled, long and slow.

"I just want you to know that I love you so much and I never thought that I could be so happy. I owe everything to you."

She tried to kiss him, but he held her shoulder gently to stop her.

"No. I need to tell you this because I've done you so much wrong and I can't live my life with you until this is off my chest and my debt to you is cleared."

Rhys gazed gravely and steadily into her eyes.

"Rhys, what you talking about?"

Her face clouded over as she tried to figure it out. He was starting to scare her. What had he done?

"When you started out. The money you lost. It was me."

Her eyes darkened as she listened in disbelief at what she was hearing. "What?"

Rhys cleared his throat, choking back emotions as he knew how much he was hurting her by telling her.

"I stole it from you. I hated you for that photo. I was doing a lot of coke. It's not an excuse, but in my sick brain, I blamed you for my fucked-up career, life, everything."

He sniffed back tears. This was destroying him.

"But I nearly lost everything. Gwen had to lend me money," she said in a daze.

"I know, *cariad*, and I am *so* sorry," he said sorrowfully.

She sat there for an age.

"Why fifteen thousand?" Her voice was monotone and cold.

"I sold the pieces and invested the money. That's what I've made on it for you."

She nodded as she took in the information.

132

"Get out," she said softly

"But…"

Oh, *Christ,* Ariana, Rhys thought. No, please, give me a chance.

"Out," she repeated more forcefully.

"Ariana!" Rhys pleaded.

"I told you, never to lie to me again and you did, so we're done. Go!"

She was now shouting at him.

Rhys broke down. This couldn't be the end. They'd moved on so much since then. He wasn't the same man he was then.

"Ariana, please. It was so long ago; you can pay Gwen back. I love you."

Ariana sobbed, "Just go, Rhys, get out of my life and leave me alone."

She stomped out of the studio and into the cottage kitchen slamming the door behind her, leaving Rhys to pack a bag and get out of her life.

Rhys was a mess and Gareth was worried. He'd been at the boathouse all evening but insisted on sleeping on the sailboat that the family owned, in the harbour. Beth had tried to get him to eat some dinner, but he'd just pushed around the lasagne on his plate. She'd offered to go speak with Ariana, but Rhys didn't want them becoming intermediaries for him. He needed to sort it with her when she'd calmed down a bit.

Gareth was concerned he might drink and was trying his best to persuade him to sleep there with them, for as long as he wanted.

"No, I can't," Rhys kept saying.

"I'll go to the boat. It'll just be for a night. I'll sort it."

"If you're sure."

Gareth reluctantly gave him the keys. It was getting late.

"Day or night, Rhys, I'm here for you," Gareth reminded him.

Rhys hugged his brother hard.

"I love her, Gareth," Rhys said huskily, sniffing.

"I know, and she loves you too. You'll work this out. Keep trying and don't give up hope."

Rhys smiled weakly at him and left to walk the track, up past the restaurant at the top of the hill, which was closing, and then down to Freshwater Bay harbour, where the sailboat was moored.

Ariana had never cried so much. How could he have done that to her? *The nasty, dishonest, conniving bastard!* He could burn in Hell for all she cared. All this time, he'd known that he'd robbed her blind, and he hadn't had the courage to tell her. A leopard doesn't change its spots, she told herself. Rhys *The Rat* Morgan was still the same deceiving character he'd been all those years ago in that hotel room, she stewed angrily as she threw the pan of pasta into the bin.

But then, she reasoned, after she'd calmed down and had a cup of Gwen's chamomile tea, he'd been so different since he'd been back. He'd done this years ago, when he was using coke, and he obviously regretted it now. He'd been trying to put things right by telling her the truth. They were so happy. She thought he was the one for her, forever. *Arrgghhhh!*

What was she going to do? Pay back Gwen the five thousand, that was for sure. And so she went, all through the night, oscillating between anger and forgiveness, for the most infuriating man that she still loved, tossing and turning in bed with the pillow beside her that still bore a hollow dent where Rhys' head had once lain.

"How much for the Penderyn?"

Rhys sat in the back bar of The Lobster Pot Inn, they were still serving, just about. If he was going to drink, it may as well be the best malt they had.

"Four pound a measure," the girl on the bar answered.

He didn't know her, but he hadn't been in there since he'd been back, and she was what, twenty? He suddenly felt old, and very alone.

"How much for the bottle?"

It sat on the shelf directly in front of him, three-quarters full.

"Err...let me check."

The girl went off with the bottle and reappeared a couple of minutes later. "Fifty quid."

Rhys got his card out and paid for the bottle.

The bar server brought the bottle down off the shelf and got him a glass, and Rhys poured himself a full glass of one of Wales' finest malt whiskies. He stared at it for the longest time. The glass sat there on the counter. One drink and he'd feel so much better, he thought. One drink and I'll be destroyed, he countered.

But without her, what did he care? His whole world was gone. It meant nothing. If he didn't touch it, he had a chance to sort things in the morning, a tiny voice in his head reasoned hopefully. As his impulses and willpower warred against themselves, the full glass of whisky sat untouched. He flicked on his phone. No notifications. No messages. He found her number and tried to call her. It went to voicemail. She was still furious with him.

"You drinking that, or taking it on a date?" Marcus, the charming tenant of The Lobster Pot, asked him from behind the bar.

"We're closing now, so drink up and piss off, yeah."

Rhys looked up and stared angrily at him.

"Great *fucking* customer service skills, man."

He walked out, kicking the barstool over. The full glass and the bottle of whisky stood untouched on the counter.

"Tosser," Marcus grumbled as he carefully tipped the glass and poured the whisky back into the bottle, looking around shiftily to see that no one saw him placing it back on the shelf behind the bar.

It was two o'clock in the morning and sleeping on the boat had not proven to be the best of ideas. Sleep had totally eluded him thus far. He boiled the kettle in the small galley kitchen and took a mug of fruit tea with him up onto the deck to look at the stars and to think.

A car's lights flashed as it moved slowly down the hill from the restaurant. He thought it looked like a sports car. It was very late to have people driving around the village. Probably some young kids, using the restaurant car park for what the locals called 'a park and ride,' he assumed.

He was now relieved that he'd resisted the whisky, but it would have been so much easier if he'd knocked it back and drifted into a drunken dead-to-the-world sleep. As it was, he had tossed and turned thinking about what he could do, until he abandoned sleep at two o'clock and headed up on deck. He'd even checked to see if she was online, if Luc could help him out now. But no, this was no time for playing games.

He looked out at the water beyond him and the stars in the June night sky. He wasn't much of a sailor, not like Gareth, but he'd like to take Ariana out on this one day. Maybe, his brother could teach him to sail it? He smiled as he remembered her holding his hand on that Art trip.

He needed to see her first thing in the morning, he resolved. Sit down and talk to her calmly, tell her how much she meant to him, try to make it right again. He looked out, up the hill towards the restaurant. Gareth had managed to patch things up, and look at him and Beth now. They were doing great. There was a light still on in the restaurant, he noticed.

It looked yellow. He looked more closely; strangely, the light seemed to be flickering.

Was that smoke? *Fuck!* He panicked. The restaurant was on fire.

Getting off the jetty and onto the harbour, he punched in Gareth's cell number, getting a groggy pick-up, finally.

"The restaurant, I think it's on fire. Call the fire brigade and come up here.... What? Alys? Get Beth to try and get hold of her on her phone. Come up with the keys and in the meantime, I'll try and smash my way in."

Rhys ended the call, rushed back to the boat and found a fire extinguisher and a hammer, before sprinting up the hill to the restaurant.

When he got to the car park, he saw the smoke billowing out from the kitchen area and yellow flames licking the back door on the inside. He went round to the front door and tried smashing his way in with the fire extinguisher, hammering the glass-paned door. It wouldn't budge. It was new and made of reinforced glass. He tried a window by the deck. It was much older, and he smashed the extinguisher into it with all his might. It cracked, and he whacked it again, making a hole in it big enough for him to get through. He felt his shirt rip on his back as he pushed through the jagged glass, but he rushed on into the smoke-filled restaurant.

Inside, the fire alarm was going off and there seemed to be no one about. The restaurant itself was still clear, but the acrid smell of burning oil filled his nostrils.

"Alys? Alys!" Rhys shouted out for her.

He screamed in Welsh and English, hoping that she'd hear.

"Tân! Fire! Cer allan! Get out!"

Thick, black smoke was building from the kitchen area as he pushed through the restaurant to the stairs. They were in front of the kitchen where the fire had taken hold; he could see the angry yellow flames in the corner, but he couldn't deal with that now. He needed to find Alys. He thought vaguely about the gas cylinders and the stoves. He had to get her out. Now. Racing up the stairs, he pushed through the smoke that was now swirling into the first-floor hallway. He knocked on all the doors and tried them, none so far were locked and the rooms he entered were all empty, as he tried each in turn. He had no idea how many of the letting rooms were occupied.

"Fire!" he kept shouting frantically, again and again at the top of his voice until his vocal cords finally gave up in the smoke that was now beginning to creep up from the floor and the stairs.

"Get out now!"

Alys emerged, sleepy and confused, with earplugs around her neck. Rhys took hold of her and rushed her down the hallway; she was barefooted and wearing a T-shirt and shorts.

"Owww!" she screamed as her feet burned from the heat of the floor.

He lifted her into his arms, her hands around his neck, legs out to the side, as they made their way towards the stairs. His lungs began filling with the hot acrid air as they descended into thick black smoke, the fire was now taking hold in the restaurant. He staggered on with Alys clinging desperately to him. He moved unsteadily, down the final steps, shielding her against the vicious flames that were now licking up against him, burning and singeing his clothes, shooting needles of hot, searing pain up the side of his arm and head.

At the bottom step, he moved quickly out of the fire's way, then tried to orient himself in the thick black smoke as to where he thought the restaurant door had been. He looked behind him, huge yellow flames danced up the walls. Struggling to breathe, he staggered forward away from the flames in the dense smoke, trying to avoid the booths, chairs and tables as he went.

They had nearly made it across the restaurant when his legs suddenly gave way and he stumbled to the floor. Alys screamed as she felt Rhys buckle from under her. He sank to his knees coughing, trying to get under the smoke, which was now a little lighter but still left his lungs feeling like they were about to explode. Alys shrieked and scrambled around on the floor, pulling at him, to follow her. He moved shakily with her, crawling on the ground, moving one knee, then the next, following the main passageway between the tables towards a flashlight that they could now see beaming through the smoky fog.

Suddenly a pair of strong hands reached towards Alys. They moved fast, rushing and throwing her towards the window where she climbed through into the car park. Gareth disappeared and re-emerged a minute later, dragging his brother by the shoulders. Then with Alys helping, Gareth got him through the jagged window. Rhys was outside, but lying on the ground, overcome by the noxious fumes.

Ariana was woken up by Gwen who had come into the studio and was trying to wake her. She was confused. What was Gwen doing here? Was she ill again, Ariana wondered as she came to?

"Get dressed," she told Ariana. "You need to get to the hospital. There's been a fire at the restaurant."

"What!" Ariana gasped.

"They've flown Rhys to Swansea," Gwen told her.

"How? What happened?"

"He went in to get Alys out. He's hurt, Ariana. I don't know how bad. You've got to get yourself over there now. Gareth's coming by to take you. Get dressed."

Ariana pulled her knees up to her chin.

"*No!*" she screamed, her head on her knees, this can't be happening.

She sprung up and threw on her jeans and a shirt, stuffed her feet into a pair of trainers and grabbed her bag, rushing up the lane to meet Gareth's car.

This was her fault. Why hadn't she just forgiven him? He'd taken the money years ago; why did she have to be so angry? He was trying so hard. Now, this!

God, please make him be alright. Please. Please. I'm sorry to have to ask again, she begged silently. I'll never ask for anything else. Just this. This once. She prayed hard into the night sky, hoping that some higher power might hear her.

Gareth's pickup truck drove up to her at speed and stopped when he saw her shadow on the side of the lane. Gareth called his parents en route to Ariana's and told them what had happened and where Rhys was. He'd taken Alys, who was unharmed but in shock, back to the boathouse, and Beth was taking care of her. The fire brigade was at the scene and had the fire under control, but the place looked a mess. He didn't want Beth to go up and see it, so he called Paul to get up there if he could. They'd worry about the restaurant in the morning.

Gwen insisted on going to the boathouse too, to help out, and had left in her car after Ariana. Madog was staying behind at the farm to milk and look after Jake. He'd try and get over to the hospital as soon as he could. He promised to call Owen and let him know too.

"Oh, Gareth," Ariana could hardly speak.

He nodded at her and turned the truck in the space by a gate.

"I love him so much."

The words came out eventually. He put his hand on her knee.

"They've taken him straight to the Burns Unit. He was unconscious from the smoke. Luckily, there were no guests staying or it could have been much worse."

She fetched a tissue out of her bag and mopped her eyes.

"Ariana, he saved Alys. If he hadn't have gone in, who knows what would've happened to her."

Beth took Alys to the sofa, sat her down gently and wrapped a blanket around her. She was in shock but unharmed. Beth put the kettle on to make her some tea then opened the large bi-fold door and ventured out onto the deck of the boathouse. Above her, on the clifftop, she saw her beloved restaurant, La Galloise, lit up a sulphurous yellow, billowing out thick smoke. Flames spat out from the kitchen side. When she saw that, she knew that the roof would go soon. The place would be a wreck. It was all over. She was still in shock herself, she realised.

Needing to keep it together for Alys, she went back inside and shut the door in case the smoke drifted down. On the human scale of it, all that mattered was that Alys and Rhys were alive; *but* Beth wondered, was it *so* selfish for her to shed a tear for the destruction of all her hard work and dreams?

CHAPTER SIXTEEN

Rhys was still in surgery getting his burns treated when Gareth and Ariana arrived. The hospital team were removing the melted clothes and assessing the damage down the right side of his body. They were keeping him sedated to control the pain, the nurse told them, as they waited for him in the recovery area.

Ariana was shaking uncontrollably. She was in shock and wracked with guilt and worry as she waited. Gareth could empathise, he had felt the same with Beth when she had her ectopic surgery. He held her, comforted her and let her cry it out; then found her some sweet tea to drink.

Ellen and David arrived a little while after, and Ariana broke down again, apologising to Ellen for the row that Ellen didn't know about, and didn't make any sense to her.

"Whatever was said or done is in the past now, *cariad*. Rhys needs you to be there for him now, and you are. He loves you. We all do," Ellen said to Ariana, holding her chin up tenderly.

"Diolch Ellen." *Thank you,* she whispered.

It was mid-morning by the time they could get in to see Rhys. He was in his own side room, sedated and asleep. His face was totally wrapped in bandages, although the nurse told them only the right half of his head had been burned. She said he'd got one third-degree burn on his right shoulder and may need a skin graft on that. In addition to his head and face, there were more second-degree burns down his right arm where the clothes had melted onto his skin as he'd brushed through the flames on the stairs and two nasty gashes along his back that were now stitched up.

He needed to rest, keep his fluids up; he was on an antibiotic drip and his wounds needed to be dressed and checked regularly.

Ariana sat in a daze, holding his hand, through the day and into the evening, not letting go. Ellen came and told her to go get some sleep. David offered to book a hotel for her near the hospital, but she wouldn't leave him. She sat in the chair by his bedside and waited for him to come round, to come back to her again. The nurses let her stay and offered her a blanket and a pillow.

In the middle of the night, Rhys stirred and moaned. Ariana leaned over to his masked face and whispering softly that she loved him, he returned to his sleep. She couldn't even kiss his lips, she felt so hopeless.

She brushed her lips over the back of his left hand. The nurses had put his ring on his bedside table, and she put it in her pocket to keep it safe for him.

It was morning. Ariana must have dozed off because she startled awake, as she felt Rhys' hand move. He was stirring and seemed to be in pain. She called a nurse over, and they checked his vitals and his drips.

"We're going to need to wean Rhys off the pain meds a little today and get these wounds dressed. You're welcome to stay, but he's going to be fine. Speak with him, and then go and get some rest. Rhys is going to be here for quite a few more days yet while his burns are redressed and to avoid infections. This will be a marathon, not a sprint," she told Ariana kindly.

Ariana couldn't think straight. She just stayed by his side as he slowly groaned back to the world around him.

"Ari," he murmured.

"I'm here, *cariad*."

She leaned over him, looking through the mask into the holes where she saw those turquoise eyes staring at her, unfocused.

He tried to reach, with his good arm, up to his face to free himself of the bandages.

"Shush, no Rhys. You've got burns. You need to keep that on for them to heal."

"What happened?" she heard him mutter softly.

"Do you remember the fire at the restaurant? You got Alys out. If it wasn't for you, she'd be dead."

Rhys slurred something she couldn't understand.

"Rhys, I need you to know that I love you. It doesn't matter about anything that's happened before. I'll always be here for you, with you. We're going to get through this."

Tears flowed down her cheeks as she finally managed to get the words she needed to tell him out.

He pressed her hand firmly.

"Caru ti, Ari." *Love you, Ari.*

She was finally persuaded to take up the hotel room offer. David had booked two rooms in a nearby hotel for the week, and she left Rhys with his parents in the afternoon, to take a shower and get some sleep. She'd need some clothes and a wash bag, but she managed to get an emergency wash pack from the reception and could at least brush her teeth and comb her hair. She crashed onto the bed, wet from the shower and slept through to the next morning.

The dawn broke as Paul and the last of the fire crew were still putting water on the restaurant roof to stop it from catching alight again. They'd dampened out the last of the flames, but the charred building was steaming, waterlogged and dangerous. This was no quick, tidy up job. The restaurant was gutted on the kitchen side. There'd be things to do immediately, phone calls to make, decisions for Beth regarding the staff. He was probably going to be out of work, Paul realised, as the full impact of the tragedy took hold.

"The fire investigators will be here first thing," the fire crew leader told Paul, "They'll try and work out what caused it. In the meantime, we need to keep the whole place closed off. It's too dangerous to go into at the moment."

Paul left them to it, to catch a couple of hours sleep. He vowed to be back mid-morning to speak with the investigator, and hopefully the police. He wasn't sure what had caused the fire. Everything, apart from the fridges, was shut down in the kitchen each night. Faulty wiring? An electrical appliance? Alys lighting candles? There could be any number of causes. But, however he squared this in his head, he needed to remind the police about the threats that Adam Williams and his cocaine-snorting thugs had made.

Ariana showered and was feeling much fresher after sleeping twelve hours straight. Ellen and David were staying over at the hotel too, and she met them for breakfast.

"Madog's coming over this morning. I've asked Gwen to pack you some clothes and toiletries," Ellen told her.

"That's so thoughtful of you, Ellen. Thank you," Ariana said gratefully.

"Rhys was starting to come round last night," Ellen filled her in.

"When will he be able to have the face mask off?"

"The nurse said that they'd reduce the dressings to just cover the burn. He was lucky, Ariana, most of his burns will heal quickly, they think. It's just his shoulder that's more serious."

The Morgans were now her family, Ariana realised, as she listened to Ellen and David relate to her more details of the fire and Rhys' treatment. And they were already closer to her than her own Mam and Dad.

"Let me see. Can you find me a mirror?"

The wounds were being dressed and Rhys wanted to see his face. He was an actor; his face was his fortune. How bad could it be?

The nurse looked at him.

"I don't think you should…"

"Please. I need to see."

"It's going to look worse than it is. Everything's blistered and red, but it *will* heal, Rhys," the nurse tried to comfort him, before getting him a mirror from behind the nurses' station.

He took the mirror with his left hand and looked at his face. A groan escaped from his lips. He was hideous, he thought to himself as he stared at his reflection. The right side of his face was covered in blisters, and between them, there were red swollen welts and nasty yellow pussy patches. His right ear was intact, but there were black blisters on the lobe, and also under his ear, on the side of his neck.

What horrified him most, though, was that the hair on the side of his head had burned off, leaving a large area of baldness, covered with the same blisters, puss and redness. He felt the familiar blackness descending on him. It was like a blanket numbing him, making him feel detached and empty. Lifeless.

"Ugh!'

He looked at himself. He couldn't bear anyone to see him like this. He was a freak. She'd never want him now. It was over, he thought grimly.

"Will it regrow?" he said pointing to the bald patch.

"Honestly, it depends," the nurse answered, "If the follicles heal, it'll come back normally, if they scar, it won't. You'll have to wait and see, Rhys."

The nurse noticed Rhys suddenly becoming very agitated.

"What's up?"

She took the mirror from his hand.

He saw Ariana looking for him in his old side ward. She was asking at the nurse's station and would be coming down to his new bed on the main ward any second now.

"Can you close the curtains, please? Send her away. I can't let her see me looking like this."

The nurse snapped the curtains closed around the bed and went out towards the nurse's station. She spotted the young woman, who was obviously Rhys' girlfriend, and went up to her.

"Can I speak with you for a second?"

Ariana smiled politely at her.

"I'm here to see Rhys Morgan."

"Can you come with me into the office, please?"

She directed her over to a small office with a cluttered desk, a large filing cabinet and two low chairs jammed in. The nurse sat at the desk as Ariana sat down low into one of the soft chairs.

"Is Rhys okay?" Ariana asked.

She was beginning to panic that something was wrong.

"Yes, but he's just seen his facial wounds. He's upset about them, and he doesn't want to see you," the nurse told her straight.

"Oh for goodness sake!" Ariana was exasperated.

"Let me talk to him."

The nurse looked at her steadily.

"Okay, but through the curtain, and if he tells you to go, I need you to do that for me, today. Are you happy with that?"

"Yes, of course," Ariana agreed.

She approached the curtains gingerly; she knew how hard this would be for him. Rhys was now in a ward of eight beds, she didn't want to turn this into a sideshow for the patients, but she had no choice.

"Rhys, *cariad*. It's Ariana. Let me come in," she spoke softly into the curtain.

"Ari, you can't. It's too bad. I'm hideous."

"Come on Rhys. I don't care."

"What if you're repulsed by me, Ariana? I am. And I can't have you be with a man you don't find attractive."

"Rhys, stop being a *bloody idiot*, will you. *I love you.* I don't *care* about anything else. And actually, if it means I'm not going to get jealous of the girls trying to catch your eye *every* time we go out, well then, you know what? *I'm glad.*"

"Ariana!"

"Come on, Rhys, let me in."

Rhys lifted himself out of the bed with his drip and tried to move the curtain with his left hand.

Ariana saw the movement and pulled the curtain to let herself in. She stood before him and looked at his face for a minute.

"*Ahh,* I've seen worse Saturday night in The Lobster Pot," she joked as she studied him closely.

"The blisters will go down in a couple of days, Rhys. And that redness will heal," she reassured him.

He sat down on the side of the bed, dejected. He groaned and turned his wounded face away from her as she moved up too and sat with him on the bed. Reaching her arm around him, she drew him to her breast. His chest heaved as she carried on regardless. Holding him tight, rocking him, she comforted him like a child, stroking his back, his wounded face buried in her chest as he battled back from the dark place that was threatening to engulf him again. Ariana would keep him from there. He knew that now.

"Thank you," he finally whispered to her, thick with emotion.

"Rhys, I've wanted to do this, ever since that night on the bridge. And I'm never going to let you go."

She breathed gently on the top of his head, still holding him to her.

"But I'm so ugly."

"Never to me, Rhys. You were lucky, you could have lost your ear or your nose, and you don't need a skin graft on your face, they've said."

"What about my hair? I'm not sure if it'll grow back." Rhys said flatly.

"So, you go cue ball for a while. I'm sure it's not the first time. Pretend you're in an army film," she said chipperly. "If you want, I can stick the clippers across it."

He looked at her dubiously, there was *no way* he was about to let her loose on his hair.

"How can you still love me like this?"

He meant it.

"How can I not?" she answered, kissing him tenderly on his damaged cheek.

He sighed and let her comfort him, feeling how big her heart was and how much she loved him with every touch.

Beth walked around the wet, charred ruins of La Galloise with the fire investigator, Gareth, Paul and the police detective that had been assigned to the case. They were wearing hard hats and boots, assessing the damage. The fire investigation team had been over everything already with a fine-tooth comb.

Beth was in tears. It was heart-breaking. She was trying to hold it together, but Gareth knew how much this was hurting her.

"Are you any the wiser as to what happened?" Beth asked.

"We're not a hundred per cent yet. We'll write the report and then the detective will discuss it with you. In the meantime, we need to get the structure safe, so you can go in and get what you need."

The investigator was a little reticent to answer. His job was to look at the causes of the fire and he'd talked to the detective about that. He was pretty sure it had been started deliberately. The witnesses he'd spoken to reported thick black smoke and yellow flames. A clear indication that a fuel source had been used. The gas tanks hadn't combusted, so it could be an external source. The kitchen window was smashed and there were remnants of five glass beer bottles on the floor inside the wooden kitchen door that the chef confirmed hadn't been there when he'd locked up. He said he'd left the restaurant clean and clear. The fire investigator also found tiny fragments of newspaper around that area. Had that been doused and thrown in to support the ignition? He suspected that quite a bit of petrol had been poured in through the window onto the kitchen floor, then it looked like petrol doused rags in glass bottles had been thrown into the kitchen to ignite it.

He was sure that there was one seat of the fire, one point where it had started. The fire had gone up the kitchen door and spread, heating the air and convecting up to the ceiling, before spreading along the beams in the ceiling space. The v-shaped pattern up the sidewall and inside of the remnants of the kitchen door indicated that the fire had spread up from there. He thought that there'd also been a point of ignition as the fire caught the oil in the deep fat fryers.

The kitchen side of the building was the most badly damaged. The far end of the restaurant had smashed windows, where the men had gone in to rescue the trapped woman, but the restaurant and the rooms at that end were mainly water and smoke damaged, though the stairs were burned.

While it sounded like arson, in these cases he took extra care. It was sometimes an inside job to get the insurance pay-out. Particularly for failing businesses. La Galloise was booming, but you never could tell. It was up to the detective to look into that. Any debts, financial pressures that would make them torch their place.

The detective had looked up the report that Beth had made about the malicious threat to the restaurant. He knew Adam Williams of old, a small-time coke dealer, thought he was the dog's bollocks; nasty bastard. Drove round in a white Mercedes sports with private plates; laboured on a building site during the day. Had done a two-year stretch in his mid-twenties.

"We'll be paying a few house calls, Beth. Leave this with us," Detective Bryn Davies told her as he examined the scene.

"Phone your insurance company, sort what you need to do with the business, customers and staff, and we'll be back in touch soon," he said, as he made his way back with her to his unmarked car.

"Oh, just to eliminate things, can you send me all your bank accounts for the last twelve months?"

Beth stood with Paul and Gareth in the car park, watching the detective leave.

"He's not thinking that we did…"

"No. It's standard elimination. He's not stupid. He knows this is an outside job, but they've got to follow up all the leads or the defence will have a field day," Paul answered definitively, putting her a little more at ease.

"What now?"

Beth looked at the ruined restaurant, drained and beaten.

"Poor Evan, what would he say if he saw this now?"

She turned to Gareth and broke down. He held her as she wept.

"Sorry Paul," she said finally as she calmed down and tried to control the tears that she'd been bottling up.

"Well, in my army days, when we had a crisis, we'd hunker down and get a plan together. This isn't going to beat us, Beth. I know we've discussed the place in the harbour. You and Gareth, go home and have a minute together. I'll come down and we'll have a coffee, work out what we need to do next. I think it may mean bringing your Lobster Pot timeline forward a touch."

Rhys told the detective everything he knew. He'd gone up on deck sometime after two and had seen the yellow light on the kitchen side of

147

the restaurant, and then the smoke. He'd called Gareth, who told him that Alys was still in there, and he'd grabbed the fire extinguisher and hammer. Unable to smash the new restaurant doors, he'd succeeded in smashing a restaurant window and he proceeded to go and check upstairs, getting Alys out. She'd been fast asleep with music playing in her ears and hadn't heard the fire alarm.

He was one brave young man, Bryn thought, as he wrote the sequence of events down carefully. Gareth, his brother, had corroborated much of what Rhys told him. His injuries didn't look so bad. He'd seen a lot worse in his career. The pretty boy'd have a sore face for a bit, but he'd live, he thought to himself.

"So, tell me about Adam Williams?" he asked. "You know him?"

He was studying Rhys' reactions carefully.

"Yeah, he was in school with me."

The detective noticed a flinch. He knew Adam quite well, he was certain.

"A mate?"

"Mmm. Kind of. But haven't seen him 'til he showed up a few weeks ago. I've been in Los Angeles for quite a few years and we lost touch when I went to London when I was eighteen."

The detective made a quick note. He believed Rhys' account.

"He wasn't a happy bunny. Some bother at the restaurant between you and him I heard?" the detective fished.

Rhys told him about what he'd seen, the drugs in the toilets and the car park deals and the confrontation outside when they'd asked Adam and his pals to leave.

"Beth reported it to the police," Rhys said.

"Did you hear him make any threats?" Bryn probed.

"Uh-huh. Said the place was a dump and should be torched."

"Anything else?"

"As I said, I couldn't sleep so when I went up onto the deck of the boat at two in the morning, I saw a car coming down the road from the restaurant. It had lights low to the ground, like a sports car. It was dark, I didn't see the colour of the car."

"You sure, Rhys?"

"Yeah. Thought it might've been kids, you know, using the car park for a bit of... *privacy*."

The detective grinned and stopped writing.

"Thank you. Anything else you remember, doesn't matter how small, let me know, okay?"

He handed him a card with his contact details on it.

Alys came a week after the fire to the hospital to see Rhys, on her way back to Paris. Her room, on the far side of the restaurant, had been one of the least damaged areas from the fire and they'd retrieved some of her things, including her passport.

"Thank you, Rhys. I owe my life to you," she said to him as she sat down in the chair by his bed.

She was still in shock about the fire.

"If you hadn't've carried me and shielded me from the flames, I don't know what would've…"

Her voice cracked and she teared up a little.

Distracting attention from herself, she handed him a tin of chocolate muffins she'd made.

"Hope you can eat them with those dressings on," she said, concerned.

"I'd pull them all off to have just one crumb of your cakes," Rhys joked kindly.

Rhys could tell that she was shocked when she saw him. How many others would react in horror when they saw him as he was now, he thought? Alys didn't stay long, she was getting the train to Bristol to fly out to Paris, but promised to come back soon and see him in Freshwater Bay.

Owen visited later that evening after Ariana had gone back to the hotel to rest.

"Chocolate muffin?" Rhys offered, holding out a tin that he struggled to open with one hand.

Owen opened it for him and they each helped themselves. The cakes were heavenly; moist light sponge with an unctuous grenache centre.

"I take it that Ariana didn't bake these," Owen asked, his mouth still full of cake.

"Alys," Rhys confirmed.

"Did I tell you; I want to marry that girl?" Owen joked as he savoured the last crumbs.

"You did say," Rhys replied, "When you were eating her chocolate mousse."

"Seriously, Rhys. You're a hero. She'd be dead if it wasn't for you."

"I thought your face'd be worse," Owen said studying his injuries carefully.

The blisters were healing but his face was still bright red with patches of seared welts.

"Give it a few weeks, and the girls'll be throwing their knickers at you again," he teased.

Rhys stared at the square tiled ceiling. He'd always taken his appearance for granted. His whole career, everything he'd achieved, little as it was, had been built around the way he looked. How would he cope now? They said he'd been lucky, there'd be no permanent scarring, but what if the doctors were wrong? His face was a mess at the moment. What if it stayed like this?

"Been doing a lot of thinking, Owen."

He turned his head to his brother.

"Well you've had a bit of time to, I s'pose," Owen replied flippantly.

"The night of the fire, Ariana and I had a fight. I nearly lost her. We're sweet now, but I never want to risk that again. I want her with me, forever. Do y'think she'll want me like this?" Rhys asked his brother, pouring out his deepest fears.

"You can be such a *vain idiot*, you know that?"

His eyes met Owen's.

"I'm thinking of asking her to marry me. If she says yes, would you be my best man?" Rhys asked his brother tentatively.

Owen cocked his head; his face cracking into a broad smile.

"Always, Rhys. I'll always have your back, no matter what. You know that, *right?*"

Rhys nodded and feigned a play punch on Owen's arm.

He hoped she'd say yes to him. He wanted to do it properly. Take her somewhere special. Life really wasn't so bad. He could live with a battered face and a bald patch. It could have been a lot worse. He'd build that house, and someday soon, he hoped, he'd live there with Ariana, and maybe down the line even have some little Finns of their own.

CHAPTER SEVENTEEN

The plan they formulated was simple. Beth would put the permanent staff on leave for a week, and then Paul would mobilise the chefs and get them ready to prepare and run the restaurant in the Lobster Pot Inn. Marcus had left, he'd shut the door and walked out, leaving an empty bar and a whole heap of filth behind.

It was grotty beyond belief. The floors in the bar were sticky from layers of spilt beer; crisps and food were ground into chewing gum stained carpets. And the toilets, *ugh*! Beth thought as she looked around the place with Paul. This was an industrial cleaning job. Not what she needed, but the only solution to keeping things afloat. The kitchen fridges had nasty surprises in them too with plastic tubs growing a whole manner of dubious moulds in them. They were a nasty health hazard.

Paul and Beth had got on the phones and cancelled bookings and suppliers. Now they'd need to clean, then drive their customers back here to The Lobster Pot. Fair play to Rhys, she thought, he'd offered to develop a social media campaign for them. He had nothing else to do whilst he sat in hospital, he said. He just wanted photos. She sent him lots of food snaps. Best not take any pictures of this place just yet, she considered as she pulled her foot off the sticky carpet. Not unless she wanted to be immediately closed down.

The detective was still working on the case. The fire investigator had confirmed deliberate arson in his fire report and the insurance people were in touch with the police. Beth had been eliminated from enquiries and there was an active investigation into Adam Williams, although Bryn, the lead detective, was only partially confident. They had CCTV footage of Adam's Mercedes entering the car park. Unfortunately, it didn't cover the back-kitchen area and the car had disappeared off camera. And there was only circumstantial evidence when they pulled him in. The four jerry cans they found in his garage, and the traces of petrol in the boot of his car were explained away. He strimmed gardens for cash, apparently. The list of his gardening clients he named, all conveniently confirmed that when the detective phoned them. Even the one that lived in a third-floor flat in town. Adam Williams was a slippery bugger, and Bryn knew that the evidence was too flimsy. It wouldn't stand up in court without more solid evidence from an informer or someone who'd heard Adam bragging or talking about what he'd done. He quietly put the feelers out. If Adam blabbed in earshot of his guys in any pub this side of Swansea, he'd have him. He put him under surveillance. And if he didn't get him for this, his lucrative little side-line would certainly come to a grinding halt soon, and then he'd have him banged up again for a good stretch for supply.

Beth was still speaking with the insurance company. They'd come out immediately and paid her upfront for the stock she'd lost, which was a massive help and would fund the Lobster Pot move. Then the wrangling began in earnest. At one point, she was despairing, thinking that they wouldn't pay out. Luckily, with Gareth's direction, she'd got a fire assessment plan in place before she'd opened the restaurant, there were CCTV cameras with footage of the car rolling into the car park at quarter to two, and all the regulatory fire prevention was in order, based on the age of the building. With the fire investigator's report and corroboration from the police, she was hopeful that there would be a sizeable settlement for the restaurant. Paul had helped them assign tasks, and Gareth was handling the building aspects. He was favouring a total rebuild and she was inclined to agree. This was a tragedy, but she was determined to start fresh and make their business even more successful.

It had taken two weeks for the doctors to be happy with the way he was healing, but Rhys was finally coming home.

"Can we stop in Holyguard on the way?" he asked Ariana as she drove their car back through the Swansea traffic.

"Sure."

She parked up and waited in the car until he emerged from the barbers.

"You look hot," she flashed him a smouldering smile as he got into the car.

"Ya think?"

His heart leapt.

He pulled the passenger side sunscreen down and looked at himself in the mirror. His hair was evened up now, closely shaved at the back and sides into a fashionable fade haircut, with the top left a little longer, combed over. Much shorter. But better, he thought.

"At least I don't look like a cat who's had stitches anymore," he said, still examining his hair closely.

He was going to be fine. His face had settled down. The blisters had gone and were now just reddened spots where the burns had been worst.

152

The doctors confirmed that there'd be no permanent scarring on his face. The only area he needed to keep dressed and sterile was the third-degree burn on his shoulder. That would take time and more outpatient appointments, maybe even a skin graft. But he could deal with that. All in all, he'd got off lightly.

"Okay, Brad Pitt, let's get you home."

She smiled at him sexily, "I've missed you *so* much."

She turned the key in the ignition, then remembering, she squirmed in her seat as she dug into the front pocket of her jeans.

"Still want this?"

She was holding his Claddagh ring.

"Ah, I've been looking everywhere for that," he exclaimed taking it from her and slipping it back on his finger.

"I didn't want to tell you, but I thought it'd got lost in the hospital."

He leaned over to her and brushed her lips lightly.

"Thank you."

He sat back and breathed in deeply as she reversed the car out of the bay to take them home. He was back on terms with the woman he loved.

Gwen greeted them when they arrived in the cottage, embracing Rhys warmly, forgetting about his bad shoulder.

"Croeso adre." *Welcome home.* "My favourite boy."

Ed the Dead was there too, apparently he'd just popped round for a cup of tea and a chat, again. Ariana looked at Gwen's flushed face and Ed's slightly dishevelled appearance and sniffed a fib.

Gwen put a pot of balm in Rhys' hand.

"I've made this 'specially for you. There's a couple more pots, so put plenty on twice a day," she told him, "Now you don't need antibiotics, put this on your face and head and it'll stop any scarring."

It was an ointment of raw honey, olive oil, comfrey, marshmallow root and witch hazel bark.

"Thanks, Gwen."

She watched them retreat into the studio and shut the door. Gwen went back to the kitchen to get them the food parcel she'd prepared; a chicken casserole she'd made and some fresh strawberries and cream. She went up to the door with the food, and was about to give it a knock with her free hand, but thought better of it when she started to hear noises coming from inside. She was sure that the windows would be steaming up next.

"I won't be knocking while the Shag Shack's rocking," she laughed to Ed as they retreated quickly back into the cottage.

"What's going on with Ed?" Rhys asked amused as he strolled over the cliff tops hand in hand with Ariana.

His favourite girl and his favourite view, he thought contentedly.

"God knows!" Ariana said slightly exasperated, "Gwen does like to have her men friends. Been like that since I've been around."

"Hope I'm like that at her age," said Rhys.

"You have more than me lined up and you're going over that cliff," Ariana said as she gave him a little nudge.

"Oh I'm so sorry," she said, immediately horrified, realising that it was his bad arm.

He played it up with an Oscar-worthy flinch as her eyes narrowed.

"Always the actor."

Gareth and Beth were delighted to see them when they called into the boathouse. Rhys held Finn, while Ariana and Beth poured them all glasses of homemade lemonade over ice.

"I can't believe how much he's filled out already," said Rhys making faces at Finn. Rhys had secured a big giggle and wasn't going to stop until he had another one.

"Little greedy guts, he's certainly got an appetite," Beth said, looking lovingly at her little boy.

"He'll be moving about before we know it."

Gareth filled them in on the fire and the investigation so far and they shared the plans to take over The Lobster Pot while the restaurant was being rebuilt.

"Woah," said Ariana, impressed. "You've been busy. So, how do you see the new restaurant?"

"I'm kind of thinking modern," Gareth answered.

"Two storied glassed steel structure, a restaurant on the first floor with a platform deck around, and a bar underneath. I'm not sure what we'll get through planning, but it's an opportunity to be creative. Fingers crossed on the insurance pay-out."

"Cool. And the accommodation?" Rhys asked.

"We'll keep the Lobster Pot for that. There are heaps of rooms there. Paul's going to manage it, and I'm trying my best to get Alys involved.

If we do this, I'll need her too. She was still thinking about it, but she did seem keen," Beth explained.

They had it all worked out, Rhys reflected, as he listened to them. He admired Beth's drive and resilience, although he left there feeling thoroughly exhausted.

Rhys wouldn't miss the finals of the drama competition for the world. He'd been unable to make the rehearsals while he was in hospital, and he chose this time to sit with Ariana and Lisa in the audience. They'd travelled an hour or so to the theatre, and groups of rival young farmer clubs sat in mobs through the audience, whooping and cheering their friends on. The atmosphere was lively, and Ariana and Rhys laughed their heads off at the sketches as they were each performed in turn. There was pantomime cows, lots of sheep and farmer gags, and the humour was definitely teenage, veering towards the unspeakable on the odd occasion.

"How was the Prom?" Rhys asked Lisa quietly as he sat next to her.

"Fine," she replied looking at the stage, her cheeks flushing.

"Sweet," Rhys said, grinning.

Aled stole the show again, Mai did a valiant effort in spite of a fluffed line and Dan put in a stalwart performance as the television presenter.

They sweated as the results were announced. Second place. Not bad for a play that sucked a couple of months ago, Rhys thought. A bit more polish and a slightly stronger script, and they would ace it next year. If they'd have him directing. He hoped they would.

When the evening ended, they all took selfies together and stopped at the McDonalds on the way home for burgers and the inquest, raking over their performance in minute detail. They were chuffed to have come second, and after milkshakes and fries, Rhys was installed as Freshwater Bay's Young Farmers' Drama Director in Residence. He'd add it to his resumé, he told them, amused.

CHAPTER EIGHTEEN

Gwen was drying out lavender, a carpet of blue stalks and flower heads covering the kitchen table, when a pale Ariana barged into the cottage kitchen and plonked herself down on a kitchen chair.

Gwen was busy snipping and stripping the plants, laying the prepared seeds onto large trays to dry in the sun, watching as Ariana slumped herself flat over the table, head dramatically in her hands, on top of the lavender, sending stalks flying to the floor.

"Ariana Jones, you going to tell me what's up or am I going to be looking at the top of your head all morning?" Gwen sighed after a full three minutes.

Ariana reached into the back pocket of her jeans and pulled out a white plastic stick, holding it up high into the air for Gwen to see, her face still flat on the table.

Gwen studied the two lines.

"*Ahhh.*"

"Yes... *Oh God!* Gwen! How could I be so stupid!"

Her head bobbed up momentarily but was back down again, buried in the lavender, which began to fill her nose.

"I thought you were on the pill?"

"I was. I am! Maybe I was a little... lapse when I was first with Rhys ... I took it a little late a couple of times," she said about to sneeze.

"Ariana!"

She sneezed.

"Don't be mad!"

Her teeth chewed over her bottom lip.

"Does Rhys know?"

Ariana looked steadily at Gwen. "No."

"Don't you think you should tell him, honey?" Gwen suggested gently.

"How can I? He's just getting over his burns and..."

"Do you want the baby?"

"Oh yes."

Ariana didn't hesitate.

"Then? I don't follow..."

Gwen looked at her, confused.

"Look at us!" Ariana despaired. "He's going to do a teaching course in September. We live in a shed. *Sweet Jesus*! We're' hardly *stable.*"

"Ariana!" Gwen scolded her for cussing.

"Sorry, Gwen."

"If a *stable* was good enough for *sweet Jesus*, then I'm sure you two will find a way through this."

Ariana raised an eyebrow.

"You've a bathroom, kitchen and wifi. That's more than Mary and Joseph had," she added dryly.

"Thanks for that," Ariana snapped caustically.

"Life always has surprises, *cariad*. It's how you deal with them that counts," Gwen advised.

"I've booked to see the doctor. I need to discuss my options. It's less than twelve weeks, I think. There may still be time."

"Oh, Ariana. Are you sure?"

Gwen went over to her and put her arm around her shoulders.

"No," she said honestly, looking up at her Gran.

"You're not your mother and you're not your father. Don't be put off by *their* failings. You've always had so much love in your heart. Bringing up a child is never easy, but if anyone can do it, you can, my girl."

Ariana nodded silently.

"But, what about Rhys?"

Gwen shrugged and patted her on the shoulder.

"Talk to him."

Rhys had been building up to the right time since he'd been out of hospital. He'd rehearsed every line and delivery of. When she wasn't there this morning, in the gallery, it had totally thrown him. She hadn't said she was off to town. And Gareth was waiting for them in the sailboat. The food and all the things they needed for a night on the boat was safely stored away.

He called her on her phone. "Where are you?"

"At the cottage."

Ariana was by the garden gate about to walk over the clifftops.

"Can you get to the harbour?" Rhys asked, relieved.

"Yes, I'm leaving now. What's up?"

"It's a surprise."

Yes, it certainly is, she thought miserably, as she started on the path over to Freshwater Bay.

When she got to the harbour, she saw what he'd planned. He'd packed clothes, food and bedding. He'd persuaded Gareth to sail them. His kayak was on the boat. Rhys was taking her to the island across the bay.

If Rhys had known that Ariana hadn't been in a small boat since the ill-fated Art trip and that she was suffering from morning sickness, he may have rethought his plans. He had tried hard to make today special, and Ariana, in turn, tried her best to be grateful and respond enthusiastically to the surprise. It was really sweet of him to have done all of this, she thought. He was a good man and she loved him so much.

They sailed in calm seas across the bay. Ariana sat quietly on the deck, looking out at the sea and the cliffs, trying to quell the panic inside her by thinking through her options. She looked across at Rhys, steering at the helm with Gareth's direction. He was a different man to the one he was even a few months ago. But, she reminded herself, he'd been so depressed he'd nearly killed himself back then. What if Rhys didn't want the child or wasn't ready for such a big commitment? She was determined not to bring an unloved baby into the world. She'd lived with *that reality* all her life. If it hadn't been for Gwen, her life with her parents would have been pretty miserable. The question *was,* did she have enough love to bring this baby up alone? And could she live her life alone with a child, without Rhys by her side?

Gareth was showing Rhys what to do in case he had to sail the boat back. It wasn't far to the harbour and Rhys had sailed before, but he was no expert. The weather was set fair and calm for a week. No squalls or winds expected. Gareth would come back the next morning, in his kayak, and sail them to the mainland. What could go wrong, Rhys thought? He had this covered. He flashed her a boyish smile.

Gareth turned his kayak and waved to them before splashing out across the open water back to the boathouse.

"That man is like a seal in the water."

Rhys watched his brother go as he sat on the anchored boat by the island.

"And this is paradise. I'd forgotten how beautiful it is out here. How beautiful you are."

He got up and grabbed Ariana from behind and play wrestled her down onto the boards of the deck. He lay on top of her and kissed her ardently. She responded and they made out like teenagers in the sunshine.

After a few hot minutes, he pulled away from her.

"Let's go for a swim to the island."

"A swim wasn't quite what I had in mind when you got me all hot and bothered just now," she teased, looking at him curiously.

"Have you packed our togs?"

"I found a bikini. Do you need it? Can't we skinny dip?"

"Rhys!"

"Ari, the only thing that'll be looking at you out here will be the seals."

"Precisely."

She won out on the swimwear, and they changed and plunged into the water, swimming for a while before making their way to the shoreline of the island.

They climbed up the beach and over the rockpools, where they sat, drying out, on a large, warm smooth stone a few metres above the shoreline, the highest point on the island. With only seabirds and seals for company, and with Ariana leaning against his chest, he looked out at their world; the harbour and Freshwater Bay across the shining waters in the distance.

"Ariana?"

"Hmm?"

She was deep in troubled thoughts about what to do. Should she tell him or should she just sort things out quietly so they could carry on with the way things are, like this, in perfect contentment? She wasn't sure she could go through with any procedures, and certainly not alone. She loved this child growing inside her already. But if he didn't want it, what would she do? She cast her eyes out to the sea. No, she thought determinedly, if he doesn't want this baby, I will do this alone.

"You know how much I love you," he grazed his lips over her sea-salted hair.

She did.

"I love you too," she said softly, a touch sadly.

He inhaled and moved himself to look at her. He took both her hands in his and with their fingers interlaced and a deep breath, he launched into his well-prepared lines.

"Ariana, you saved me. Turned my life around and made me a better man. I need you with me always... Ariana, will you marry me?"

His deep turquoise eyes bore into her heart as he looked at her, the burns on his face now only the faintest marks of life.

159

She gazed back at him, searchingly. What could she say? She couldn't deceive him, after everything they'd been through, and their vows to be truthful.

"I can't," she whispered, her voice thick with emotion.

"What?"

"Why not? Speak to me. What's wrong?"

She shook her head, took her hand away from his and put it to her mouth.

"I can't do this to you."

She got up to move. It wasn't fair to him.

He gently pulled her back to him.

"What is it, *cariad*?"

She heard his voice crack as he said it. She was breaking his heart too.

"I was going to tell you, but I didn't want to trap you," she said finally.

Rhys was confused. What had she done to trap him? Suddenly, it dawned on him. He held her face in his palms and lifted her gaze gently to look at him.

"Ariana, are you trying to tell me that you're pregnant?"

She nodded, teeth grazed over her bottom lip, she stared at him blankly, unsure.

He was silent for a moment before his face suddenly broke out into a huge, wide smile.

"That's fantastic!"

He covered her mouth passionately with a kiss and she gasped. Her eyes blinked back the shock and elation as she began to realise that he seemed *more* than happy, thrilled even.

"It is?"

"Yes! Don't you think?"

Their eyes met and she studied them, trying to find what he really thought.

"I do. I want our child, but it's going to change everything, and we're *really* not ready for this," she hedged tentatively.

"Who is, Ari?" he reassured her, *finally* understanding.

Her eyes betrayed the root of her fear. That the child would be an inconvenience to him, like she always felt she was to her parents.

"I promise you, Ariana, that this child will be the centre of our world, no one will love them more than us."

"But we live in a shed," she threw at him weakly.

"For now. But we're working on that."

"You're starting the teaching course?"

He batted it deftly away. "It's only for a year, we can get by."

She sighed. Could this work out after all?

Rhys whispered into her ear, "Ariana, marry me. Not because of the baby, but because of us. We're made to be together. You've always been the only one for me. I'm crazy about you. And I think you can tell, I'm crazy about this baby too. How could I not be?"

She studied his eyes. He was all in.

"Yes," she said finally, breaking into an uncertain smile.

"Yes?" he repeated, not quite sure, she'd agreed.

"Yes. Rhys. Yes!" she laughed, showering him with soft kisses. "Yes!"

He punched the air, shouting loudly to the rocks below.

"Hey, seals! I'm going to be a dad!"

Ariana threw her head back and erupted into laughter as he conversed with his new friends.

"It was at the farmhouse, I think. I'd been a little careless with the pill," she admitted as they started to process the news and the changes that were happening to them.

"I think I'm about ten weeks along."

        "Ah, the bluebells."

Rhys cast his mind back fondly.

"Hmm. The perfect place for our first little baby in our new home. That night was all *my* doing if I remember right, but I don't regret it."

He held her tightly.

"Ariana, this is the best day of my life."

        "Mine too," she mouthed into his neck seductively.

He kissed her feverishly and led her back to the shoreline, back to the boat and an afternoon of lovemaking and laziness in the mellow July sun.

EPILOGUE

The October leaves were golden and glorious in the woods around Cae Môr farm, as family and friends gathered at the large marquee set up in the field below. Mr and Mrs Morgan descended from their decorated horse and trap and walked down to meet their guests. Rhys Morgan, ten months sober, expectant father, trainee teacher, online sales and web designer took his final leap of faith and had just married the love of his life, Ariana Jones. They'd been married in Freshwater Bay chapel and Ariana had asked David to take her down the aisle. Her mother and father were away, cruising the Caribbean. They'd booked it ages ago and couldn't cancel, they'd told her. It was one of those things.

Ariana was dressed in a long, flowing boho bridal gown with vintage lace and a Forties style v-necked bodice. Her hair was dressed with rosebuds and piled up loosely off her neck. She cut a willowy figure with a discernible neat little bump at the front. Ariana was a little embarrassed about this, but no one else seemed to care. Rhys said it made her look even sexier, and that was impossible because she was already the sexiest woman on the planet, in his eyes. He wore a light wool waistcoat with a paisley patterned shirt. The hair on the right side of his head would always be patchy, but he'd grown used to that now. He kept it close shaved and it didn't matter to him anymore. And he was the proudest man in the world today.

Ellen and David hosted the wedding, and Beth, Paul and Alys fixed up the catering. A band was set up on a flatbed trailer, one of Rhys' mates from school. It was going to be a long evening of music, food and fun.

Dr Owen Morgan was best man and had been anxious all day, waiting for the dreaded moment when he had to deliver his speech in front of the guests. This was not his thing at all, and he'd had to resort to a quick snifter to quell his nerves. The irony of that, as Rhys' sobriety sponsor, was not missed on him, and he chewed a piece of mint gum assiduously, hoping that Rhys, sitting next to him, wouldn't smell the shot of whisky on his breath. The speech went off fine in the end, and afterwards, he wondered what the week of stress he'd just gone through had been about.

He had some news too. He'd signed up with a Paris rugby club and was leaving Cardiff for the season, almost immediately. When he shared the news with Rhys, he told him he fancied a change. He only had a few playing years left and wanted to travel a bit now he'd completed his studies. Moving to Paris would also help clarify the Julia situation. He'd overheard her talking with Ellen about what wedding she'd like, which was crossing all kinds of lines. He'd realised then that she obviously couldn't handle their arrangement, even though he'd been very clear with her, and he needed to end it for good.

If Alys Edwards had any inkling that Owen Morgan had just signed a year of his life away to a foreign rugby club, on the prospect that he planned to be spending a lot more time with her, she would be wobbling even more than those delicious elderflower champagne jellies she'd made for the wedding feast.

Since the accident, she'd been in constant touch with Rhys and Ariana online. She'd been having nightmares and anxiety issues, and they were helping her through it.

She looked stunning today, Ariana thought. She was wearing a magenta Grecian style dress that fit tightly around her full breasts. Owen's eyes had been glued on them all day. That fact had not gone unnoticed by Julia either, who had gone sulkily back to Cae Môr farm alone, early to her bed. Owen would, no doubt, pay for that later, Ariana smiled to herself.

"Can you help me, please?"

Paul turned around from the buffet line, where he was directing his trainee chefs. They were in full flow, serving Jamaican Jerk Chicken, his own Grandmother's famous recipe, for the evening revellers. In the corner, a tall woman was leaning and swaying precariously off the top of a chair, stretching to clip back into the corner, a piece of the tent's inside dressing that had come away. He hastily put down the large pan of rice and peas and rushed over to help her, as she looked as if she was about to fall. He held her legs, steadied the chair and helped her down.

"Let me do it."

She was tall, but he was a good deal taller and he stood on the chair and clipped it in effortlessly.

"Thank you."

She introduced herself.

"Hi, I'm Vanessa. Vanessa Cartwright. I own the marquee."

"Paul. Paul Campbell."

"Saw you today, Paul. You ran the catering like a military operation. Great job!"

He smiled. If only she knew, he thought.

She handed him her card.

"Ever wanna work with me, give me a call."

She flashed a bright broad smile at him and walked away leaving him to watch her very cute ass in tight jeans move sassily across the marquee and out of the tent door.

Outside, under the festoon lights that were strung up around the marquee, couples filled the outside dancing space. Dan smooched with Lisa; he was leaving early the next day to start his thirty-two-week basic training with the marines. His dad was proud, but still perplexed as to why he'd chosen the Navy corps, not the paratroopers, like him. It was meant to be a bitch of a programme. Paul hoped he'd get through it.

David took Ellen up to dance, and Gwen sitting alongside them, grabbed Ed's hand, pulling him up too for a turn on the floor.

"You're not dead yet, Ed. Come on," she persisted when he tried futilely to refuse.

Beth Morgan, dancing with her husband, spotted a certain six-foot five rugby player with his arms wrapped around a certain curvaceous, auburn-haired, patisserie chef. Van Morrison's Moondance was playing and there they were, Alys thought, dancing under the harvest moon. She really had tried to resist him. She'd been disappointed to see him sat by his television presenter girlfriend all day, though she seemed to have disappeared now. And in spite of Alys' protestations, he'd dragged her up for a dance and now here she was.

Owen's hands gently caressed her bare back and her full breasts were now pressed up a little too closely against the rugby player's huge torso for her liking. Her heart beat fast as she moved with him slowly around the dance space, feeling that this was all kinds of wrong. He felt her heart thumping too and he caged her to him, trapping her even closer as his lips threatened to graze gently along her neck and up to her lips, where he stole from her unexpectedly, a hot, open-mouthed kiss. It ended with the music and a hard, stinging slap across Owen's face. Alys freed herself from the prison of his substantial clutches as Owen swore and rubbed his cheek.

"I think your girlfriend's keeping your bed warm," Alys told him bluntly, rubbing her hand to rid herself of the sting of the slap.

As she stomped out of sight, Owen followed her with his eyes, wondering exactly what he'd done wrong.

"I like her," Ellen whispered to David as they moved to sit back down.

David shrugged, smiling. "About time he got his just deserts if you ask me."

Beth gazed up at Gareth, willing him to stay for one more dance before they went home to relieve the babysitter. It had been a tough few months, but her restaurant at The Lobster Pot Inn was now open for business until the new La Galloise was rebuilt. Gareth was working on that now that the insurance had finally paid out. Adam Williams had not been charged as yet but Beth didn't think he'd show up again. Everyone knew what he'd done, and as he was banned from the Lobster Pot, there was nowhere for him to get a drink in Freshwater Bay.

Rhys and Ariana Morgan were nowhere in sight. But look a little further and they could be found slow dancing too. They'd snuck off unnoticed, down the lane, then the track, to their tumbledown house. Their future life and dreams now fused and formed firmly together in the meadow by the ancient oak tree with the bluebell bulbs sleeping silently in the autumn earth beneath their feet.

"I told you I'd come to you, Bianca," Rhys murmured as they held each other under their own piece of moonlight.

"Yes, Luc you did."

ABOUT BOOK THREE

The Freshwater Bay Series continues in Book Three:

Their Just Deserts: Alys and Owen

ABOUT THE BOOK

When International rugby sports star Dr Owen Morgan, first sees Alys Edwards, he tells his brothers that she's the woman he's going to marry. He's the team strategist, the playmaker, the psychologist after all, and he *always* gets what he wants. Unfortunately, pastry chef, Alys doesn't seem to have read the playbook on this one. She's living in Paris, enjoying a summer of love with the man of her dreams. So, when Owen Morgan comes into her life, can he win her heart? And will he find a way for them to be together or will they always be just friends? Unexpected career changes test their resolve as life draws them back to West Wales and Freshwater Bay.

Paul Campbell, chef and ex-paratrooper, is ready to move on with his life. When he meets Vanessa Cartwright he's sure that he's finally found his soulmate. But how can they both move forward when their past lives are still haunting and holding them back?

Read the first chapter free

THEIR JUST DESERTS - FIRST CHAPTERS

Freshwater Bay - Book Three
Alys and Owen

CHAPTER ONE

Freshwater Bay - Book Three
Alys and Owen

"Dance with me."

Owen Morgan, professional rugby star, and what Alys Edwards classed as an Adonis of a man, was holding out his hand to *her*, a humble pastry chef with a wobbly ass and flabby thighs, and asking *her* to dance with him.

And *boy*, did he look hot, she thought, as she gazed up at his tanned, rugby-rugged face and those piercing blue eyes of his that were now bearing down directly on her.

"No. You've got a girlfriend," she told him firmly.

He didn't deny it or try to explain her away. She'd seen him with her before Julia had slumped off on her own to bed.

"It's you I'm gonna marry, Alys Edwards," he seductively flirted, flashing her a dazzling smile.

"When I first tasted that chocolate dessert of yours, I told my brothers, *she's the one*."

Alys screwed her nose as she looked up at him. He was full of it.

"Hmm. My chocolate mousse gateau, yeah? You *do* know that I lace it with secret drugs. And I'd say, right now, you're obviously trippin', pal."

The six-foot-five man-mountain smiled but continued to tower over her; he was not taking no for an answer, it seemed.

"You can't help it," she carried on, "There's actually a love drug in the chocolate. You're doped up to the eyeballs and totally under my powers. In fact, you're the tenth proposal I've had this evening."

He dropped another delicious smile that made her heart thump loudly and won him that dance.

"Come on, Alys. Take a risk. It's Van Morrison. What's the worst that could happen?"

"I could get my eyes scratched out by your girlfriend in a catfight?"

"I'd protect you from her," he whispered into her ear as he took her hand, sweeping her onto the outside dancefloor, set up by the side of the wedding marquee.

So, there she was, in spite of her protestations, with Owen *Greek god* Morgan, slow dancing, his arms wrapped tightly around her, to Van Morrison's Moondance *beneath the cover of October skies,* in a field near Freshwater Bay.

This *had* to be full-moon madness, she reasoned. Her heart thumped as Owen's huge arms caged her closer to him, pressing her against his muscular torso. Bending his head down towards her shoulder, she felt his hot breath lingering on her collarbone. It moved deliciously along her neck and then gently upwards until she felt his mouth sweeping softly over her, delicately tasting her lips. She really did try her very best to resist his charms, but as his mouth fell upon hers, she opened and deepened their kiss, aiding and abetting in it becoming a hot, passionate tangle of all kinds of wrong. The music and then the kiss ended, abruptly, with a sharp slap, right across Owen Morgan's cheek.

"I think your girlfriend's keeping your bed warm for you," Alys huffed, rubbing her smarting hand guiltily. She *had, after all,* been a willing accomplice.

One girl in his bed and another on the dancefloor, Owen Morgan, just who do you think you are, she humphed? And more importantly, who do you think I am? Grumbling to herself, she stomped away to check that the catering team had packed up everything properly.

When she'd agreed to help Beth and her deputy Paul with the food at Ariana and Rhys Morgan's wedding she hadn't expected to hook up with Rhys' brother, Owen, the Best Man. She just prayed that no one had taken a photo of them or tagged her. The last thing she needed when she got back to Paris from her weekend in West Wales was to face questions from her boyfriend, Leo.

"What did I do wrong?" asked Owen, rubbing his face and turning to his eldest brother Gareth, who was coming off the dance floor with his wife Beth, Alys' best friend.

Gareth sniggered, "You're the Doctor of Psychology, I'll let you work that one out.".

Julia, lying in her black lace negligee, snapped the light on when she heard his footsteps coming up the creaky farmhouse stairs and into the bedroom. As soon as he opened the door, a little unsteadily and a little drunk, she ambushed him.

"What the Hell were you doing, dissing me like that in front of your mother?" she hissed, winding up to pounce again.

"*What the fffk? Shhh!* Julia, they'll *hear* you," Owen whispered a little too loudly as he tried to quieten the situation. His parents were a couple of bedrooms down the hall from them and he knew from experience that the sound in the old farmhouse carried.

"I don't care if I wake the *whole house*. You didn't need to embarrass me *like that*."

"Like what?"

He hoped she hadn't seen him kissing Alys.

"Telling your mother that we weren't getting married."

"Well we're not," he answered bluntly.

Julia's lips tightened.

"You were telling my mam how you couldn't marry anyone in a marquee in the field because you've got posher friends than my brother. *With better shoes.* Have you any idea how that sounds, Julia?"

She stared coolly at him; did he *really* not get it?

"When you gonna start treating me properly and start committing to me as a girlfriend?" she flung at him finally.

This misguided delusion that Owen had, that they had some form of *'open arrangement'* needed to end once and for all, she decided. He called it a *'no-strings-attached'* relationship. Well, she'd been pulling his string on and off for over a year now; she was *way* beyond being his booty call. His commitment phobia had gone on for long enough.

Owen sat on the side of the bed and tried to take her hand, but she slipped them both under the duvet out of sight and wriggled further down under the covers.

"Look, Julia, you know it's gonna be tricky for me over the next few months," he began, trying to close the conversation so he could get some sleep.

This was not what she needed to hear right now.

"I can't believe you did that," she snapped, *"Paris!* What on earth made you sign with them? You didn't even *ask* me."

She was a regular presenter on the couch for Britain's top-rated evening talk show. She even read the sports on the ten o'clock news. These gigs didn't just fall from the sky. They took a lot of work to get. Going to the right parties, meeting the right people, having the right image. The right boyfriend. It was important. It was how you got on, got the breaks. And for *that*, she needed Owen on her arm. She wanted him as her celebrity sports star boyfriend, a massive hunk of man muscle with a winning smile and a witty line. The perfect companion for martinis with media producers.

"You *know* how I *need* you in London, hun," she wheedled.

"Julia, I am never gonna live in London and I can't commit to a relationship right now."

She huffed, turning over and pulling the covers up to her chin.

"What's wrong with London? Beats *frickin'* Freshwater Bay any day. *Ugh!* Sheep shit, mud and *bloody* rain. I *hate* Wales."

Owen blew out a deep breath, undressed and slipped in beside her, his back to her as he turned off the light.

He decided that this might not be the best time to tell her that he'd done a deal that week and invested a large chunk of his hard-won sports star earnings, buying The Lobster Pot Inn, Freshwater Bay's main hotel. Best never to tell her either that he'd also snapped up Gareth and Beth's boathouse as a place to live after the rugby ended. He was off to Paris for a few months, but his home would always be here, whether *she* liked it or not.

"Saw you getting on very well with a certain rugby player last night, Miss Edwards," Beth shot a mischievous smirk at her best friend Alys.

It was Sunday morning and Alys had been staying with them at the boathouse over the wedding weekend. It was just into October and still warm enough to sit out. Enjoying the sea air at the outside table on the boathouse deck, they were eating scrambled eggs and toast, whilst Gareth was feeding Finn in the highchair inside, giving the two friends a little girl time.

Alys smiled back cheekily and took a sip of her freshly squeezed orange juice.

"Hmm, I think Owen was a bit drunk last night."

Beth grinned at her.

"He's into you, Alys."

Alys looked at her friend in disbelief. It was ridiculous. No way. Not with *her* fat ass and thunder thighs.

"Take it from me. I was watching. That boy was appreciating your assets most of the day," Beth added conspiratorially, nodding towards Alys' ample chest.

"No!" Alys giggled, "With his hot girlfriend there too?"

"Yeah, I'm not sure what's going on with Julia Johnson, Gareth tells me it's a booty call kind of thing. An open arrangement where they hook up from time to time. But from what Julia was hinting at to me last night, she doesn't seem to have got the memo on that one."

"He'll get his just deserts with her, then," Alys surmised, finishing her eggs, "He's a bit of a tart if you ask me. Guys like him, it's all about the challenge. Once they win the woman, it's game over. Move on to the next."

"I saw that slap you gave him. That musta hurt."

Alys covered her eyes with her hands and peeped through.

"I know! It connected and stung my hand after. Oh well, at least I left my mark on him, eh?" she added, biting her bottom lip. She hoped he'd forgive her. He was a tough boy; she was sure he must have worse than that every Saturday on the rugby field.

They chatted about Freshwater Bay and their friends. Alys and Beth had both worked together as chefs in London until Beth met Gareth Morgan, an architect, and left the city to run a restaurant in this pretty little village on the West Wales coast. Alys had helped her out a few months before, when Finn was born.

Whilst Freshwater Bay seemed like a slice of paradise to most people, the place had its problems like everywhere else. While Alys was staying, the restaurant had been set on fire by a disgruntled drug dealer. They were now rebuilding it and doing their best in the interim to run the restaurant from The Lobster Pot Inn, a rundown hotel on the harbour front.

"How you doing Alys, since the fire?"

"I'm healing but I still have nightmares," Alys answered truthfully.

She'd been in there, asleep, the night La Galloise got torched, a terrifying experience. Rhys Morgan, Owen's brother, had pulled her out through the flames and saved her life. She still bore the mental scars of

171

that terrible night, as did Rhys. Going through the fire together had bonded them and they were now firm friends. It was wonderful to see Rhys and Ariana finally get married yesterday, *and* with a baby on the way.

"It helps talking about it with Rhys."

"What a turnaround that boy's had," Beth agreed.

She looked up from the boathouse deck to where La Galloise used to stand, above them, high on the clifftops. The site had been bulldozed clear and Gareth was overseeing the new restaurant design and build. They'd shared the plans with her earlier on, it was going to be fabulous. Wall to wall glass with huge panoramas of the sea. The first steels were going into the ground next week.

"How you going to cope now that Finn's moving around?" Alys asked.

Designed again by Gareth, the boathouse was a Scandinavian style open-plan house on the water's edge. But it was also one *total* toddler hazard and Beth had told Alys secretly that they'd just found out that baby number two was going to be coming along in a few months' time.

"Gareth's been super-busy," Beth told her.

"I'll say," Alys smirked.

Beth hadn't been sure if she would ever be able to have children, so to get pregnant again so quickly after Finn had been a bit of a shock.

"No!" Beth answered, colouring up.

"Busy with *the builds*. We've had to get contractors in," she explained. "With three projects we can save costs by doing them together. The restaurant, Rhys and Ariana's farmhouse renovation and the family house for us that we're planning in the field near the chalet complex."

"You're not staying here, then?" Alys asked, surprised.

"This boathouse was great for the two of us, but we're gonna need more space."

Beth looked at her seriously for a moment.

"Have you thought more about what I said last time you were here? About coming back home and working with us. We'd love to have you as part of this team, Alys. You're my wing-woman, you know that?"

"You've got everything at The Lobster Pot covered for now though, yeah?" Alys replied.

"Well, yes, while we're rebuilding, but after that, it's a blank canvas. We've got the lease and now there's a new owner who's up for fresh ideas. I think we should run it as a hotel," she hinted.

Alys considered things a bit more.

"Beth, I'm not sure. I've met someone in Paris. His name's Leo and he's French."

Printed in Poland
by Amazon Fulfillment
Poland Sp. z o.o., Wrocław

50551936R00103